Mrs Moore

Scholastic Literacy Skills

D0243606

Comprehension

Ages 8-9

Photocopiable skills activities

Authors Gordon Winch, Gregory Blaxell and Helena Rigby

Editor Roanne Davis

Assistant editor David Sandford

Series designers Joy Monkhouse and Rachael Hammond

Cover illustration Gerald Hawksley

Illustrations Beverly Curl

Designed using Adobe InDesign
Processed by Scholastic Ltd, Leamington Spa

Published by Scholastic Ltd, Villiers House, Clarendon Avenue,
Leamington Spa, Warwickshire CV32 5PR

Printed by Bell & Bain Ltd, Glasgow

Adapted from original material entitled *Read Well* © Gordon Winch
and Gregory Blaxell published by Martin Education of Horwitz House,
55 Chandos St, St Leonards 2065, NSW, Australia

Text on pages 5-21 and 92- 128 © 1998 Helena Rigby
© 1998, 2002 Scholastic Ltd

 4 5 6 7 8 9 0   4 5 6 7 8 9 0 1

British Library Cataloguing-in-Publication Data
A catalogue record for this book is available from the British Library.

ISBN 0590-53885-3

Contents

The publishers would like to thank the following for permission to reproduce copyright material.

(page 104) HarperCollins Publishers USA for the use of an extract from *No Roses for Harry* by Gene Zion © Eugene Zion 1958 (1958, HarperCollins USA).

(pages 120, 101, 102) Dave Higham Associates for the use of extracts from *Charlie and the Chocolate Factory* by Roald Dahl © Roald Dahl 1973 (1973, Puffin); *The Twits* by Roald Dahl © Roald Dahl 1982 (1982, Puffin); *A Birthday For Frances* by Russell Hoban © Russell Hoban 1983 (1983, Hippo Books).

(page 93) Barbara Ireson for 'John and Jim' from *Over and Over Again* © Barbara Ireson 1978 (1978, Beaver Books; 1984 Hutchinson Books Ltd).

(page 94) Karla Kuskin for 'The Witches' Ride' from *Dogs and Dragons, Trees and Dreams* © Karla Kuskin 1980 (1980, HarperCollins).

(page 100) Sheila Lavelle for 'Ursula Bear' from *Ursula Dancing* by Sheila Lavelle © Sheila Lavelle 1977 (1977, Hamish Hamilton).

(page 96) Brian Lee for the use of his poem 'Bones' from *A First Poetry Book* © Brian Lee 1979 (1979, Oxford University Press).

(page 92) Sarah Matthews for the use of 'Crayoning' by Stanley Cook from *A Very First Poetry Book* edited by John Foster © The Estate of Stanley Cook 1984 (1984, Oxford University Press).

(pages 98, 99) Reed Consumer Books Ltd for 'The first chick' from *Penguin's Progress* by Jill Tomlinson © Jill Tomlinson 1991 (1991, Mammoth); 'The Owl Who Was Afraid of the Dark' from *The Owl Who Was Afraid of the Dark* by Jill Tomlinson © Jill Tomlinson 1991 (1991, Mammoth).

Every effort has been made to trace copyright holders for the works reproduced in this book and the publishers apologise for any inadvertent omissions.

Introduction

Comprehension means 'understanding' and, in its narrowest sense, comprehension material tests children's understanding of what they read. However, true 'comprehension' goes much deeper than this. Therefore the main objective of the *Scholastic Literacy Skills: Comprehension* series is to foster reading and comprehension skills in the widest possible sense, so that children not only learn how to read, and to extract information from a variety of types of text, but also begin to appreciate the enjoyment and learning they can gain from a range of books. While the children are working on activities in this series, they will become more aware of the different features of various types of text genres, and will begin to understand how organisation of language, choice of vocabulary, grammar, layout and presentation all influence meaning.

The complete series consists of five photocopiable skills activity books, one for Key Stage 1/P1–3 (ages 5–7) and one for each of the years of Key Stage 2/P4–7 (ages 7–8; ages 8–9; ages 9–10; and ages 10–11).

Working at text level

This series of comprehension books gives children opportunities to work at text level. It is well known that text-level work gives an essential context for work at sentence and word levels. It is also an essential part of the meaning-making process, which is at the heart of effective reading.

Typical activities in text-level work are identifying main points, awareness of organisation and linguistic features of different text genres, differentiating fact, opinion and persuasion, and awareness of tense, mood and person in writing and how they affect meaning. You will find all these aspects of comprehension, and more, represented in the *Scholastic Literacy Skills: Comprehension* series.

Reading strategies

In order to learn to read well, a reader must be motivated. The variety of reading material offered by this series will ensure that children's interest will be captured so that their reading confidence will be developed.

Testing comprehension can never be a precise art. Any reader brings to new text a considerable 'baggage' of opinions, knowledge (or lack of it) and personal experience. All of these factors are bound to affect how that person responds to what they are reading and how much, or what type of, information they will retrieve from it.

To be able to understand a text fully, the reader will need to have acquired the skills of detailed (close) reading, and search reading (including skimming and scanning). To answer questions on the content of the text, the reader will require retrieval skills to locate and select the appropriate information, as well as communication skills to express responses verbally or in writing.

Close reading

Reading a text in detail gives the reader a clear understanding of what it contains. The passage should usually be read more than once, particularly if its content or subject matter is difficult or unfamiliar. This initial read through should allow the reader to fully grasp the meaning and intent of the author.

Skimming and scanning

Once the reader is familiar with the text and understands it, search skills are required if the information needed to respond to a particular question is to be located swiftly. The reader needs to be able to skim through the passage quickly and scan the parts of the text where the answer might lie.

Answering the questions

Answering comprehension questions can be challenging for a young reader, particularly in the early stages. It would be of value to the children if the texts, and possible answers to the questions, could be discussed in small groups before they are asked to work individually. This will help them to structure their answers and will also support any children who have limited reading and writing skills. Children should always be encouraged to answer the questions in complete sentences, where appropriate, as this will also enhance their writing skills.

Types of question

The four aspects of comprehension covered by questions in this book are literal, inferential, deductive and evaluative comprehension. Each of these tests a different facet of the reader's understanding of the texts. Explanations of these four types are given below, but it should be recognised that there is a considerable amount of overlap and that questions may sometimes fall between two or more categories.

• **Literal comprehension** centres on ideas and information that are quite explicit in a particular text. The reader is required to locate the response to a question, the clues to which lie on the surface of the text. In its simplest form, literal comprehension can be the recognition or recall of a single fact or incident, but it can also take more complex forms, such as the recognition or recall of a series of facts or the sequencing of incidents.

• **Inferential comprehension** requires the reader to 'read between the lines'. The information needed to respond to an inferential question is implicit in the text, and the reader needs to make inferences based on what has been read to formulate an answer. This type of question is more challenging, as it explores the extent to which the reader is aware of the nuances of meaning in the text. Children may, initially, need help to look for hidden clues and to link cause and effect.

• **Deductive comprehension** demands that the reader delves even deeper into the passage to make inferences based, not only on the text, but also on the reader's own experience and background knowledge. The reader is required to draw on personal knowledge and demonstrate a broader understanding of the text using links of cause and effect drawn from experience. Again, children may need support and guidance in formulating their answers.

• **Evaluative comprehension** asks the reader to make an evaluation of arguments or ideas suggested by the text. In order to do this, readers need to compare the information provided with their own experiences, knowledge or values. Answers given to this type of question depend on readers' assessment of a situation and how they would react to it, given their own inclinations and experiences. Generally, it is not possible to provide set answers to these questions, although pointers to the areas that should be covered are sometimes offered.

Using this book

The activities in this book unite the skills of reading and writing. They also involve speaking and listening as the work is discussed with the children before they make a written response. Each of the main and supplementary units comprise a reading comprehension passage followed by questions that focus on the four types of comprehension described above. The passages cover a variety and balance of eight different fiction and non-fiction genres and the activities are arranged in groups by genre. (The genre of each passage is indicated on each page.) The eight text genres are:

Fiction
• poetry
• drama
• narrative

Non-fiction
• recount
• instructions
• report
• explanation
• argument

The main units

Each of the 30 main units in this book follows the same pattern. It begins with an introductory section, which gives some brief information on the purpose or structure of the relevant genre. This is followed by a 'Before you read' section, which offers one or two questions to engage the reader's attention and raise awareness of the content of the unit. These questions could form the basis of a small group discussion before the reading task is attempted.

The introductory sections are followed by a reading passage. These passages gradually increase in length and difficulty throughout the series to extend children's reading experience and foster reading development. The reading passage is followed by about ten comprehension questions based on the text. The questions are designed to test the four main types of reading comprehension already discussed.

In the early stages, the emphasis is on literal comprehension, and appropriate answers to the questions could be discussed in small groups. The children should then be encouraged to answer the questions in their own words, using full sentences. This approach would be particularly helpful to children who need guidance in locating the specific relevant information and making the appropriate inferences from the text. Children will respond in different ways to the evaluative questions, as answers depend on their

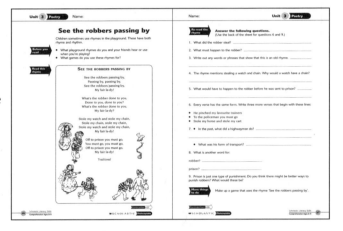

own experiences and preferences. For these too, discussion would help them to formulate responses. As children gain experience and confidence, they will become more able to work through the units on their own, with the minimum of adult help.

The final section of each unit offers suggestions for further activities, loosely related to the content of the unit, which more able children might wish to try.

Suggested answers to the questions in the main units can be found on pages 82–91 of this book.

The supplementary units

The supplementary units in this book complement and reinforce the work of the main units. They contain further examples of the genres represented in the main units – poetry, narrative, drama, recount, instructions, report, explanation and argument – thus offering the children a wider variety of fiction and non-fiction texts. As with the main units, the

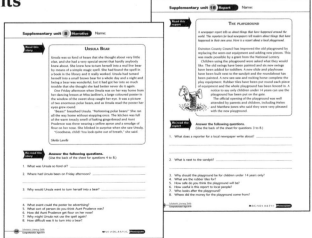

supplementary units are grouped by genre and are designed to match the target age group. Within each genre group, the passages increase in length and number of questions to offer a progression. The questions posed are balanced to give equal weight to the four types of comprehension already discussed.

Children working on one of the supplementary units should first read the passage, preferably in a small group. They should then be given the opportunity to discuss the passage and possible answers to the comprehension questions. Next, the children should answer the questions, trying always to use their own words rather than repeating sections of the text. It is important that they develop the habit of reorganising and rephrasing the information they take from a text. The ability to do this will demonstrate their understanding of what they have read. As always, questions should be answered in complete sentences where appropriate, rather than with one word or a phrase.

Suggested answers to the questions in the supplementary units can be found on pages 123–8 of this book.

The answers

All answers are laid out clearly, unit by unit. At the start of each section, a listing of question types for the passage is given, which identifies how many questions there are in each category – literal, inferential, evaluative and deductive.

Answers are given as directly as possible. Where children are likely to give a range of replies, this is introduced by the phrase 'Answers may vary', followed by suggestions of the types of points answers should cover. Where

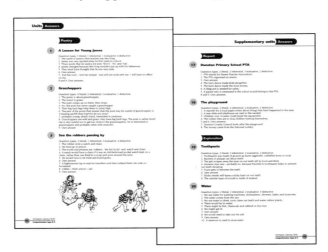

questions depend almost entirely on the individual's experience and opinions, the phrase 'Own answer' is given. Obviously situations may arise where children's answers may differ greatly from those suggested. It is usually worth checking the child's understanding and method of expression while also rejecting (though kindly) inventive or purely hopeful answers.

Poetry genre

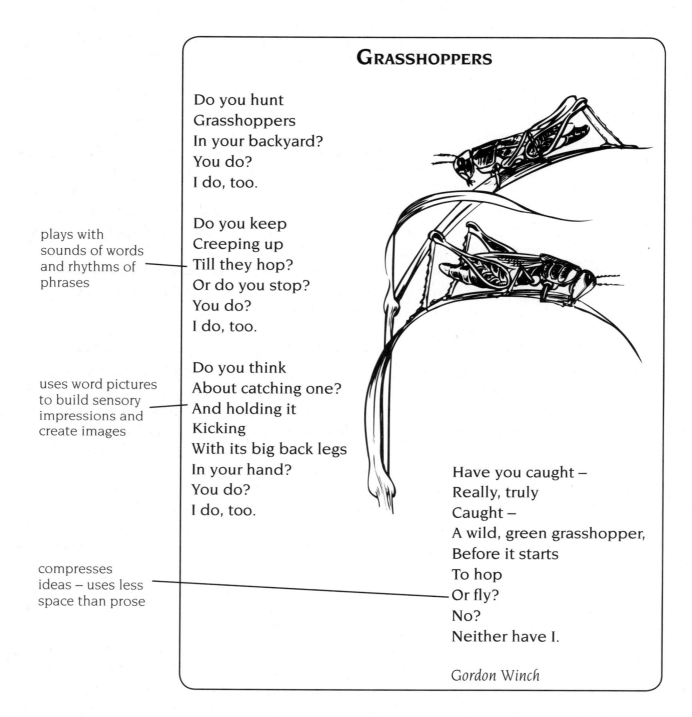

GRASSHOPPERS

Do you hunt
Grasshoppers
In your backyard?
You do?
I do, too.

plays with
sounds of words
and rhythms of
phrases

Do you keep
Creeping up
Till they hop?
Or do you stop?
You do?
I do, too.

uses word pictures
to build sensory
impressions and
create images

Do you think
About catching one?
And holding it
Kicking
With its big back legs
In your hand?
You do?
I do, too.

compresses
ideas – uses less
space than prose

Have you caught –
Really, truly
Caught –
A wild, green grasshopper,
Before it starts
To hop
Or fly?
No?
Neither have I.

Gordon Winch

Narrative genre

A CLOSE SHAVE

It was a clear morning. The sun was just coming up as we arrived at the slipway. There was hardly any breeze and it felt as if it could get very hot.

There were three of us going fishing – my dad, my best friend Hannah and myself. This was the first time Dad had taken us fishing from his boat.

Dad started the motor and soon we were speeding down the river towards the sea. When we arrived at Dad's special spot, we put down the anchor and waited for the fish to bite.

In no time at all I felt a pull on my line. I reeled it in and saw I'd caught a nice mackerel. It made me feel pretty good that I'd caught the first fish. We caught three more fish after that.

It had become very hot, and big, black clouds were starting to bank up. "I think we'd better head home," said Dad. "It looks like there's a storm coming." We wound up our lines and Dad asked me to pull up the anchor once he'd started the motor.

He pulled the starter, but nothing happened. He tried again, and again. "I'll just check the spark plug," he said. "It can get a bit dirty." He took out the spark plug and looked at it. Just then, a big wave hit us and the spark plug fell into the water!

"I don't have a spare with me," said Dad. "And that storm is getting closer." I could tell that he was angry with himself.

The sky had gone very dark and there was thunder and lightning all around. A gust of wind came across the bay. With it was a shower of rain.

"What'll we do, Dad?" I asked. I was scared. So was Hannah.

"Don't panic. I've just remembered – Mum put the mobile phone in the bag. I'll ring the coastguard. They'll help us."

In no time at all the coastguard launch arrived and they took us on board. Then they towed our boat back to the slipway. We were all really glad to get back on dry land because the storm had got a lot worse. We were all soaked through, but at least we were safe!

involves setting,

characters,

plot and

dialogue that work together to open and develop the action

presents a problem to solve

ends the narrative with a solution to the problem

Drama genre

tells a story via
the setting,
sound effects
and dialogue
between
characters

speaker's name
in small capitals;
colon

layout and
punctuation
conventions

usually in
present tense

involves what
characters
actually say

TROUBLE AT HOME

*Joshua and Luke are on the school bus on their way home. Joshua is a bit
worried because his dad has just lost his job.*

JOSHUA: I don't know what Dad's goin' to do. He's lost his job.
Company went broke.

LUKE: Went broke? So they let him go?

JOSHUA: Yeah. I don't think it's fair.

LUKE: What did he do?

JOSHUA: Drove a truck.

LUKE: It's bad luck! What's he goin' to do?

JOSHUA: Look for a job. He checks the paper every mornin'.

LUKE: Hasn't found anything?

JOSHUA: Naw! Rung up for a couple of jobs but didn't get 'em.
(He *pauses as if he is thinking of something. He frowns*) He
gets grumpy about it.

LUKE: That's what happened to my dad. When he lost his
job, him and mum started fightin'.

JOSHUA: Yeah I know.

LUKE: He went for a job today. A mate of his told him about
it. I've got my fingers crossed.

JOSHUA: I hope my dad finds a job soon.

LUKE: Yeah, it's rotten. Got to get off next stop. Hope your
dad finds somethin' soon.

JOSHUA: Me too. See ya.

Recount genre

Alphorn Chalet
Rue St Antoine
Beauville
Switzerland

19 January

Dear Abigail,
  Disaster today – it is too windy to ski! Last night there was a blizzard, which is still raging. As I look through my window, all I can see is snow blowing everywhere. Everyone is staying indoors.
  Up until yesterday the weather was perfect for skiing. Oliver and I have had skiing lessons every morning. Even Mum and Dad go to a ski class. The teachers are all very young and are great skiers. They show you what to do and then give you a chance to try. It looks easy but is often very hard work. My ski instructor says I am learning very quickly.
  After our lesson we spend a couple of hours skiing down the slopes. Dad and Mum are good skiers, so they can do the hard runs. Oliver and I just ski down the gentle slopes. We find that's hard enough for us. We still fall over a lot!
  Skiing makes you very hungry, so we always have a huge lunch when we get back to the chalet.
  I hope this blizzard blows out today so we can ski again tomorrow. If it's fine, the snow will be great.
  See you next week back at school.

Love Danielle

usually in past tense

may involve a narrative structure, for example autobiography

contains details

is usually chronological

uses action verbs

may involve personal feelings and opinions

may be personal (involves 'I' or 'we')

Instructions genre

describes how to carry out a process or procedure

lists materials needed to carry out a process or procedure

features action verbs

is usually a series of steps in a specific order (which may be numerical, chronological and so on)

is in present tense using imperatives

frequently omits definite articles

HOW TO PLANT A TREE

Materials
(what you need)
tree in pot or other container
spade
watering can
fertiliser or compost (if available)
small stake
tree tie

Tree in pot

Steps
(what to do)
1. Dig hole (larger than container) in ground.
2. Loosen soil in hole.
3. Water hole and allow water to soak in.
4. Turn tree container upside down.
5. Hold tree and remove from pot with care.
6. Place tree in hole.
7. Pack earth firmly around roots.
8. Spread compost or fertiliser around tree.
9. Water tree lightly.
10. Push or hammer in stake near tree and fix with tree tie.

Tree in hole, level with ground

Earth packed around roots

Report genre

THE FAIRY PENGUIN

focuses on a specific
subject or idea

Fairy penguins are the smallest type of penguin in the world. They live in the south of Australia and in New Zealand.

is usually in present
tense

Fairy penguins weigh about 1 kilogram and stand 30 centimetres high. Their back feathers are dark blue and their front feathers are white. They have a beak, webbed feet and flippers.

Penguins live on the land and in the sea. They are very good swimmers and divers, but they cannot fly. They eat small fish and squid.

provides facts,
diagrams and
examples to support
the subject

Fairy penguins breed on land. The female lays two white eggs in a burrow, and the male and female share the job of sitting on the eggs. When the babies hatch they are covered in white down.

At the start the mother and father bring food from the sea, but after eight weeks the baby penguins have grown feathers and are soon ready to hunt for their own food.

Fairy penguins are often in danger. They are hunted by wild animals; they are caught in nets and on long lines; if they get covered with oil, they drown. Many of their breeding grounds have been taken over by humans who have gone to live there. If their numbers become too small, these little penguins might disappear for ever.

Explanation genre

describes how something works or why something happens

is usually in present tense, using a series of steps in a specific order

involves facts

may involve diagrams

WHY THE SEA IS SALTY

The sea is salty because salt is washed into the sea from the land.

First, rain washes salt from the ground, and this salt dissolves in the rainwater before running into the rivers. When the rivers flow into the sea they carry the salt with them.

Every year millions of tonnes of salt are washed into the sea, and when water evaporates from the sea, the salt is left behind. This means that the sea contains more and more salt as the years go by.

The Red Sea and the Dead Sea are more salty than the oceans. This is because they have many rivers flowing into them. Also, they are inland seas and not very big, so the salt builds up. The extra salt in the water makes it very easy to swim in these seas.

The rain washes out the salt from the land

Salty water goes into the rivers

The rivers flow into the sea with the salt

Argument genre

puts forward a point of view

has an opening statement

has a series of reasons or evidence for the argument which may include details and facts

TRAVEL TEACHES YOU MANY THINGS

When you travel you are able to learn many things that you cannot learn at school or at home.

By travelling to other countries you can find out about the people who live there. If you are able to spend time in the place where they live you will get a real opportunity to understand many things about the lives of people in other places.

You can see what kind of lifestyles they have – what their homes are like, what they eat, what kind of clothes they wear. You can learn what types of jobs they do, how they get about and how they spend their leisure time. By walking among them, sitting near them in restaurants and buses and hearing the language they speak, you will really start to know them in a way you would never be able to from books, films or television programmes.

You can also learn a lot about yourself. How different is your lifestyle, your language, the food you eat? Could you live like them, eat the food they eat, learn their language? When you start to ask yourself these things, you will learn a great deal about others, and a lot about yourself. Travel teaches you about other people and other places. It also encourages you to think about yourself and where you live. Many of the things you experience by spending time in another country cannot be learned in any other way.

includes a closing statement which sums up the argument; usually in present tense

Assessment

Scholastic Literacy Skills: Comprehension can be valuable in helping you to assess a child's developing progress in English. Comprehension exercises test, above all, children's ability to read and make sense of text. Because the reading passages are appropriately labelled with a particular genre name, it is relatively easy to spot whether a child is less or more able to tackle and make sense of specific types of text. Moreover, by looking at whether particular questions are inferential, deductive, evaluative or literal, it is also easy to recognise areas where the child is having difficulty. In either case, there is a wide range of differentiated material to choose from in the main and supplementary units in this book, which will challenge or build confidence in most children in the primary school.

Photocopiables for assessment and record-keeping

Pupil's record and evaluation sheet
This has been designed to be completed mainly by the children. It provides a record of the units covered by each child and allows each child to indicate his or her interest, level of difficulty and level of achievement. It is useful in highlighting individual patterns of needs, interests and strengths. It also builds a strong sense of achievement in each child.

Class record of progress
This follows the class as it moves through the school, providing a record of what has been covered in each year. It can help teachers find a starting point with a new class. It also helps with progression between year groups.

Pupil's record and evaluation sheet

[Name] _____ 's record

Fill in the chart for each unit you complete.
Use these symbols, or make up your own.

Date	Unit	Did I enjoy it?	Was my work good?	Was it easy?

Teacher's comments

Class record of achievement

Unit	Title	Genre	Date
1	A Lesson for Young James	Poetry	
2	Grasshoppers	Poetry	
3	See the robbers passing by	Poetry	
4	Hare in Summer	Poetry	
5	The Fox and the Crow	Narrative	
6	King Midas and the golden touch	Narrative	
7	Katy's dog	Narrative	
8	A close shave	Narrative	
9	Catherine and the Carrot King	Narrative	
10	The genie	Narrative	
11	A narrow escape	Narrative	
12	Trouble at home	Drama	
13	The Hare and the Tortoise	Drama	
14	The haunted house	Drama	
15	First day in Year 3	Recount	
16	A letter to Grandma	Recount	
17	A letter to a school friend	Recount	
18	Scrambled eggs on toast	Instructions	
19	Tug of war	Instructions	
20	How to plant a tree	Instructions	
21	Football	Report	
22	The fairy penguin	Report	
23	Learning to swim	Report	
24	Why the sea is salty	Explanation	
25	How to find information in a book	Explanation	
26	Why there is lightning then thunder	Explanation	
27	We should look after our trees	Argument	
28	Going to school	Argument	
29	Things were better then	Argument	
30	Travel teaches you many things	Argument	

Class record of achievement

Supplementary unit	Title	Genre	Date
1	Crayoning	Poetry	
2	John and Jim	Poetry	
3	The Witches' Ride	Poetry	
4	Water	Poetry	
5	Bones	Poetry	
6	The first chick	Narrative	
7	The Owl Who Was Afraid of the Dark	Narrative	
8	Ursula Bear	Narrative	
9	The Twits	Narrative	
10	A Birthday for Frances	Narrative	
11	No Roses for Harry	Narrative	
12	Charlie and the Chocolate Factory	Narrative	
13	Treasure trove	Drama	
14	My new school	Recount	
15	Fruit and cheese kebabs	Instructions	
16	First aid for a grazed knee	Instructions	
17	Dunston Primary School PTA	Report	
18	The playground	Report	
19	Toothpaste	Explanation	
20	Water	Explanation	
21	The library	Explanation	
22	Early to bed	Argument	
23	Dental hygiene	Argument	
24	Saving wildflowers	Argument	

A Lesson for Young James

Poetry takes many forms. Many poems are quite short, but others tell a long story. The clues that show that a piece of writing is a poem are line length, rhythm, rhyme and special words. Sometimes all of these are used, sometimes just one or two.

Before you read

- What was the name of your first teacher at school?
- What special things do you remember about the person?

Read this poem

A LESSON FOR YOUNG JAMES

Young James had always had his way
In nearly everything,
Until the day he went into
The class of Mrs King.

Now James was very spoiled, you see,
Before he started school,
But when he shouted out, "I won't!"
His teacher lost her cool.

"You are at school now, little boy,
And you will quickly see
That saying 'Won't' and 'No' and 'Yuk'
Just will not work with me."

So James learned to behave in class,
He's quite a different boy.
And gets on well with everyone,
Which gives his teacher joy.

Gregory Blaxell

Continued on P23

Re-read the poem

Answer the following questions.

1. What was the name of James's first teacher? _____

_____

2. What sort of boy was James when he first came to school? _____

_____

3. Write down three words that James used a lot when he first came to school.

_____

4. Why did James change? _____

_____

5. What do you think the other children in the class thought of James when he first came to school?

_____

6. What types of behaviour by your classmates do you particularly like or dislike?

_____

7. What is meant by these phrases?

lost her cool _____

Just will not work with me _____

8. What do you remember about your first day at school? _____

_____

9. What was the hardest thing about going to school for the first time?

_____

More things to do

Write another verse for the poem or make up a poem about someone you remember from your first class in school.

Continued from P22

Grasshoppers

Poems can be about many different things and come in many different shapes and sizes. Poems often use rhyme, a particular beat (or rhythm) and special words.

Before you read

- Are there creatures living in your garden or a park near your home that scare you? What are they?
- Name three creatures that you would enjoy watching in a garden or park.

Read this poem

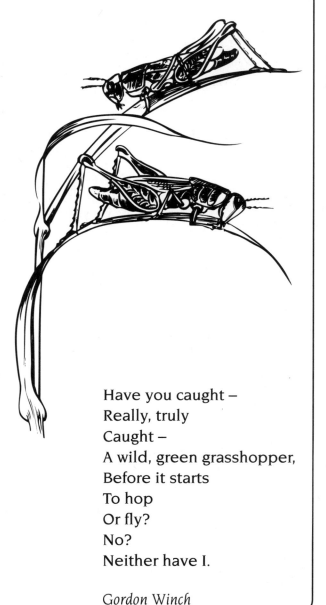

GRASSHOPPERS

Do you hunt
Grasshoppers
In your backyard?
You do?
I do, too.

Do you keep
Creeping up
Till they hop?
Or do you stop?
You do?
I do, too.

Do you think
About catching one?
And holding it
Kicking
With its big back legs
In your hand?
You do?
I do, too.

Have you caught –
Really, truly
Caught –
A wild, green grasshopper,
Before it starts
To hop
Or fly?
No?
Neither have I.

Gordon Winch

Continued on P25

Re-read the poem

Answer the following questions.

1. What insect is the poem about? _____

2. What colour is the insect? _____

3. Does the poet rush after the insects or creep up on them? _____

_____

4. Has the poet ever really caught one? _____

5. What helps grasshoppers jump so high? _____

6. Does any part of the poem make you think that the poet is a bit scared of grasshoppers? Which part?

_____

7. The poem tells you a number of things about the poet. Circle the words or phrases below that you think best describe him.

probably young   unafraid   brave   interested in creatures

  probably old   afraid   timid   not interested in creatures

8. • What does the poem tell you about grasshoppers? _____

_____

  • What does it tell you about the poet? _____

_____

9. • In what ways are you like the person in the poem? _____

_____

  • In what ways are you different? _____

_____

Continued from P24

See the robbers passing by

Children sometimes use rhymes in the playground. These have both rhyme and rhythm.

Before you read

- What playground rhymes do you and your friends hear or use when you're playing?
- What games do you use these rhymes for?

Read this rhyme

SEE THE ROBBERS PASSING BY

See the robbers passing by,
Passing by, passing by,
See the robbers passing by,
My fair la-dy!

What's the robber done to you,
Done to you, done to you?
What's the robber done to you,
My fair la-dy?

Stole my watch and stole my chain,
Stole my chain, stole my chain,
Stole my watch and stole my chain,
My fair la-dy!

Off to prison you must go,
You must go, you must go,
Off to prison you must go,
My fair la-dy!

Traditional

Continued on P27

Re-read the rhyme

Answer the following questions.
(Use the back of the sheet for questions 6 and 9.)

1. What did the robber steal? _____

2. What must happen to the robber? _____

3. Write out any words or phrases that show that this is an old rhyme. _____

_____

4. The rhyme mentions stealing a watch and chain. Why would a watch have a chain?

_____

5. What would have to happen to the robber before he was sent to prison? _____

_____

6. Every verse has the same form. Write three more verses that begin with these lines:

- He pinched my favourite trainers
- To the policeman you must go
- Stole my horse and stole my cart

7. • In the past, what did a highwayman do? _____

_____

    • What was his form of transport? _____

8. What is another word for:

robber? _____

prison? _____

9. Prison is just one type of punishment. Do you think there might be better ways to punish robbers? What would these be?

More things to do

Make up a game that uses the rhyme 'See the robbers passing by'.

Continued from P26

SCHOLASTIC **Photocopiable**

Hare in Summer

Some poems have animals as their subject. This poem, written by the Australian poet Flexmore Hudson, is about a hare.

Before you read

- Have you ever seen a hare? What other animal is it like?
- Imagine it is a hot day in summer, you are walking in the countryside and you see a hare. What would you expect the hare to be doing?

Read this poem

HARE IN SUMMER

In the little strips of shade
that a strainer-post has made,
squats a weakly panting hare.
All day he has squatted there.
Only with the shade he shifts.
As I approach, he slowly lifts
his goggling eyes, but will not run,
fearing me less than the naked sun.

Flexmore Hudson

Re-read the poem   **Answer the following questions.**

1. What season of the year is it? _____

2. The hare is sitting in the shade. What is making the shade? _____

_____

Continued on P29

3. When does the hare change its position? _____

_____

4. What happens when the poet approaches the hare? _____

_____

5. What words tell you the hare is very hot? _____

_____

6. Underline which of these three things the hare is most frightened of.

someone approaching

not having enough to eat

going out of the shade and into the very hot sun

7. Why does the hare **slowly lift his goggling eyes**? _____

_____

8. Why has the hare just **squatted there**? _____

_____

9. Why does the poet describe the sun as **naked**? _____

_____

10. What do you think a strainer-post is? _____

_____

11. What would happen to you if you were caught outside in the very hot sun and could find no shade?

_____

12. What words in the poem rhyme with:

hare? _____   run? _____

shade? _____   shifts? _____

Continued from P28

The Fox and the Crow

A fable is a story that has a message about how to behave. The story begins by telling you what is happening, and when and where it happens. This is followed by some events which lead up to one main event. This main event changes, and finishes, the story.

Before you read →

- Circle the word below that best describes how a fox behaves:

  cheerful   honest   sneaky   bad-tempered

- What sort of noise do crows make? Choose the words that best describe their call:

  tweet-tweet-tweet   screech-screech   ar-c-k ar-c-k ar-c-k

Read this fable →

THE FOX AND THE CROW

Once there was a crow who had just found a lovely piece of cheese. She picked it up and flew on to the branch of a nearby tree.

Just at that moment a fox walked by. He looked up and saw the crow sitting on the branch with the lovely piece of cheese in her mouth.

"I want that piece of cheese," he said to himself, "and I know how to get it!"

"Lovely morning," he called out to the crow. "How well you look this morning. I've never seen you looking more beautiful. Your eyes sparkle like the running stream. Your feathers are as black and as glossy as the river stones, and I know your voice is just as beautiful. Please crow, is there any chance that you might sing me a song on such a beautiful day as this?"

The crow listened. "What a nice fox he is! Yes, I'll sing for him," she thought. So she opened her mouth, but only a loud "ar-c-k, ar-c-k" came out. It really was an awful sound.

As she opened her mouth to sing, she dropped the cheese onto the ground. Quick as a flash, the fox snapped it up and gobbled it down.

"That's all I wanted, crow. But I'll give you a piece of advice. Don't trust people who flatter you." And with that he ran off into the undergrowth, still licking his lips.

Continued on P31 →

■SCHOLASTIC Photocopiable

Re-read the fable

Answer the following questions.

1. What had the crow found on the ground? _____

_____

2. Where did the crow fly to eat what she had found? _____

_____

3. How did the fox plan to get what the crow had found? _____

_____

4. What happened when the crow began to sing? _____

_____

5. The story ends with the fox giving the crow some advice. What is it? _____

_____

6. Why did the fox think that his plan would work? _____

_____

7. Why did the crow forget that if she opened her mouth, the cheese would drop out? What was she thinking about?

_____

_____

8. Which birds might sing better than crows? _____

_____

9. Crow says, **"What a nice fox..."** Do you think the fox really is nice? _____

_____

More things to do

How might the story have ended if the crow had looked down at the fox and thought to herself, "I know he's trying to trick me. I'll just fly away"? Try writing a new ending to the story.

Continued from P30

King Midas and the golden touch

A myth is an old story (a narrative) which tells of gods, heroes, imaginary men and women from the past and magical happenings. Many myths come from ancient cultures – this one is a Greek myth.

Before you read

- What do you know about Hercules, a hero from Greek myths?
- Jason was another Greek hero. Do you know the name of his ship, his companions and the treasure they were seeking?

Read this myth

KING MIDAS AND THE GOLDEN TOUCH

There once lived a king called Midas. He was very greedy and believed that the most important thing in the world was gold.

"If only…" he said to himself, "if only I could turn things into gold, I would be the happiest man in the world."

At that moment a beam of sunlight streamed into the room, and from it appeared a young man who said, "I grant your wish, King Midas. Everything you touch will turn to gold."

Next morning, when Midas awoke, he found he already had the golden touch. The chair beside his bed turned to gold as soon as he touched it, the cover on the bed turned to gold… Midas was overjoyed. He could have all the gold he wanted!

A servant arrived, carrying his breakfast. Imagine the king's surprise when the pancakes turned to gold when he touched them, the fresh fruit turned to gold, even the egg in the eggcup turned to gold!

"However will I eat?" Midas asked his beautiful daughter, Marigold, as she skipped into his room. "I will starve to death."

Marigold ran to Midas and threw her arms around him. He bent down to kiss her. Alas! Her rosy cheeks were suddenly cold, hard and yellow. His daughter had turned to gold!

Midas was overcome with grief. What had he done? At that moment the young man appeared again in a beam of sunlight.

"Have you learned anything, Midas?" he asked.

"Oh, yes," replied the unhappy king. "Gold does not bring true happiness. Take away the golden touch."

The young man granted the wish, the golden touch left Midas and Marigold came back to life. "Ah!" said Midas to his daughter. "The only true gold is the gold of your beautiful hair. I have learned my lesson."

Continued on P33

■SCHOLASTIC Photocopiable

Re-read the myth **Answer the following questions.**

1. What was the name of the king's daughter? _____

_____

2. What was the first wish he was granted? What was the second? _____

_____

_____

3. What was Midas going to eat for breakfast? _____

_____

4. What was the first problem the golden touch brought to Midas? _____

_____

5. What do you think was the worst thing that happened to him? _____

_____

6. Midas didn't think ahead. How do you know this? _____

_____

7. What clues are there that this story might be a myth? _____

_____

8. What does **I have learned my lesson** mean? _____

_____

_____

9. If you were granted a wish, what would you like most? _____

_____

More things to do
- Find out some more about Hercules and Jason.
- What would you say if you were granted the 'golden touch'? Why?

Continued from P32

Katy's dog

A narrative tells a story. It has a beginning, a middle and an end. At the beginning we meet the characters and find out when and where the story takes place. In the middle one or more things happen, then there is a crisis and at the end everything is worked out.

Before you read

- What are some good things about owning a dog?
- What do you have to consider if you plan to get a dog?

Read this story

KATY'S DOG

Katy loved her dog, Dylan. He was her very best friend. He was a mixture of breeds and a mixture of colours. He had long legs, a short tail and long hair. He followed Katy everywhere.

When Katy took Dylan for a walk he was obedient and gentle – unless Katy was in danger. Then he became a raging tornado.

One day, Katy took Dylan to the park across the road. It was a big, open park but Katy's mum could watch them both from the kitchen window. She also knew that her daughter would be safe as long as her faithful dog was with her.

Katy and Dylan were playing with a ball when two strange dogs came into the park. They were big and fierce and ran towards Katy. Dylan dropped the ball and stood in their way. Unable to get to Katy they attacked Dylan instead. Dylan was a tough fighter and well able to stand up for himself. The noise frightened Katy, but she was able to run away, across the road to her mother.

Katy was safe, but what about Dylan? Katy called to him. "Dylan! Dylan! Here boy!"

There was no answering bark. No bounding dog ran to her. Everything was silent in the park. Dylan had gone.

Katy looked for Dylan all the rest of the day. Her mum helped, and her dad when he came home. There was no sign of the lost dog. Something must be wrong.

"Maybe he chased the strange dogs and has got lost himself," Dad said. "Dylan is bright, though. He'll find his way home."

Katy did not sleep very well that night. She kept thinking of Dylan. Was he hurt? Would he ever come home?

Early in the morning she crept out of bed and went down to check outside the front door. Something muddy and rather battered was sitting on the mat. It wagged its stubby tail as Katy shrieked with delight.

Continued on P35

Re-read the story

Answer the following questions.
(Use the back of the sheet for question 10.)

1. What was the name of Katy's dog? _____

2. What did the dog look like? _____

_____

3. What happened in the park? _____

_____

4. How did Katy's mother feel about Dylan? _____

_____

5. What do you think usually happened when Katy called Dylan? _____

_____

6. Was Katy's father right in what he said about Dylan? In what ways was he right?

_____

_____

7. Why was Dylan muddy and battered? _____

_____

8. What does **he became a raging tornado** mean? _____

_____

9. Describe how Katy felt at the end of the story. _____

_____

10. How might you feel if you lost your pet?

More things to do

- If Dylan could talk, what would he tell Katy when he came home?
- Write your own narrative about a lost pet.

Continued from P34

Photocopiable

A close shave

A narrative begins by telling the reader where and when the story is happening. It contains a series of events, leading up to a main event which changes the course of the story and brings it to an end.

Before you read

What important things would you need to take if you went fishing in a boat?

Read this story

A CLOSE SHAVE

It was a clear morning. The sun was just coming up as we arrived at the slipway. There was hardly any breeze and it felt as if it could get very hot.

There were three of us going fishing – my dad, my best friend Hannah and myself. This was the first time Dad had taken us fishing from his boat.

Dad started the motor and soon we were speeding down the river towards the sea. When we arrived at Dad's special spot, we put down the anchor and waited for the fish to bite.

In no time at all I felt a pull on my line. I reeled it in and saw I'd caught a nice mackerel. It made me feel pretty good that I'd caught the first fish. We caught three more fish after that.

It had become very hot, and big, black clouds were starting to bank up. "I think we'd better head home," said Dad. "It looks like there's a storm coming." We wound up our lines and Dad asked me to pull up the anchor once he'd started the motor.

He pulled the starter, but nothing happened. He tried again, and again. "I'll just check the spark plug," he said. "It can get a bit dirty." He took out the spark plug and looked at it. Just then, a big wave hit us and the spark plug fell into the water!

"I don't have a spare with me," said Dad. "And that storm is getting closer." I could tell that he was angry with himself.

The sky had gone very dark and there was thunder and lightning all around. A gust of wind came across the bay. With it was a shower of rain.

"What'll we do, Dad?" I asked. I was scared. So was Hannah.

"Don't panic. I've just remembered – Mum put the mobile phone in the bag. I'll ring the coastguard. They'll help us."

In no time at all the coastguard launch arrived and they took us on board. Then they towed our boat back to the slipway. We were all really glad to get back on dry land because the storm had got a lot worse. We were all soaked through, but at least we were safe!

Continued on P37

Re-read the story → **Answer the following questions.**

1. How many people went fishing? Who were they? _____

_____

2. Where did they put the boat into the water? _____

_____

3. Where was the slipway located? A harbour, a lake or a river? _____

_____

4. How many fish were caught altogether? _____

5. What were the signs that a storm was coming? _____

_____

6. Do you think that Dad was worried too? Why? _____

_____

7. Why did they travel back in the coastguard launch? _____

_____

8. What could have happened if they hadn't had the mobile phone? _____

_____

_____

9. How do you think Mum felt when the family got home? What might she have said?

_____

_____

10. What do you think the title of this story means? _____

_____

_____

Continued from P36 →

Catherine and the Carrot King

A narrative tells a story. It has a beginning (introduction), a middle (complication or crisis) and an end (resolution). In the beginning, we meet the characters and find out when and where the story takes place. Then a number of things happen – these events lead to a crisis and an ending in which everything is worked out.

Before you read

- Do you like carrots? What do you like or dislike about them?
- This story is a fantasy (it couldn't really happen). Name a fantasy you have read or seen on television or at the cinema.

Read this story

CATHERINE AND THE CARROT KING

"Not carrots again!" sighed Catherine. "Mum gave me raw carrots for lunch as well. They took ages to chew and I didn't get any playtime. I hate carrots!"

Zing! Zap! Suddenly there was a flash like lightning, and standing in front of Catherine was a fearful figure. He had a carrot-coloured cloak, a carrot-coloured suit, pointed carrot-coloured shoes and – believe it or not – a crown made of carrots on his head.

"I," said the terrifying creature, "am the Carrot King, feared ruler of Carrot Kingdom. My task is to teach children who don't like carrots just how good they are for them. You are my prisoner. Jump into the carrotmobile with the others. Quickly now!"

When the carrotmobile arrived at the palace of the Carrot King, the children were led into a carrot-coloured room through a carrot-coloured door. In front of them was a long table covered with dishes of carrots.

There were long carrots, short carrots, thin carrots, thick carrots, boiled carrots, baked carrots, steamed carrots, and – of course – raw carrots.

"This," said the Carrot King, looking very fierce and peering at each child, "is your task. You must eat every carrot on this table before midday. Leave one tiny piece and you will have me to deal with! Ready, steady, eat!"

Continued on P39

Re-read the story ▶ **Answer the following questions.**

1. Did Catherine like carrots? What were her reasons? _____

_____

2. What did the Carrot King look like? _____

_____

_____

3. What was on the table in the Carrot King's palace? _____

_____

4. What task did the Carrot King set? _____

_____

5. Who do you think were the 'others' in the carrotmobile? _____

_____

6. Why do you think the Carrot King wants to persuade them to like carrots? _____

_____

_____

7. This story has two main characters. What are their names? _____

_____

8. What elements of the story show you that it is a fantasy? _____

_____

9. If there were a Carrot Queen in this story, how might she be dressed? _____

_____

_____

Continued from ▶P38

SCHOLASTIC Photocopiable

The genie

A narrative is a story that begins by telling the reader where and when things are happening. It continues with a series of events (plot), leading up to an event which changes the story. As a result, the plot can develop further or the story can come to an end.

Before you read

- What would you wish for if you were cold and had nowhere to go?
- If you found a magic genie, what would you ask for?

Read this story

THE GENIE

It was a dark, dark night. The snow was coming down and it was very, very cold. The wind howled.

"Where will we sleep tonight?" asked Kirpal. "If we stay out here in the snow we'll freeze to death."

"We could try the train station," said Scott. "When it's very cold they sometimes let us stay there."

They walked slowly towards the station. The wind was really cutting into them. They took a long time to get there. When they arrived they found all the lights were turned out and the station locked up. What could they do? They were so tired that they sat down on the steps.

Kirpal suddenly noticed a bottle lying on the ground nearby. It seemed to have a faint blue glow, so he bent over and picked it up. It was dirty, so he rubbed it on his trousers.

All at once there was a huge bang and flash and a magical figure in a glittering blue suit was standing next to them. Kirpal and Scott could not believe what they were seeing.

"Master, what do you desire? Tell me what I must do," boomed the genie.

After a moment's hesitation, Kirpal whispered: "Find us a warm place to stay for the night, please. And something hot to eat."

In a blinding flash Kirpal and Scott found themselves in a room with two cosy beds. In the fireplace a fire was burning brightly. On the table were two plates of food that steamed deliciously.

The genie stood by the door waiting for the next command.

Continued on P41

SCHOLASTIC Photocopiable

Re-read the story → **Answer the following questions.**

1. What were the names of the two boys? _____

_____

2. Was it summer or winter? _____

3. Where did the boys decide to go to look for shelter? _____

_____

4. Why did Kirpal rub the bottle on his trousers? _____

_____

5. What do you think the food on the table was like? _____

_____

6. How do you think the two boys felt when the genie first appeared? _____

_____

_____

7. What is meant by **the wind was really cutting into them**? _____

_____

8. What do you think the genie looked like? Write a short description of him. _____

_____

_____

9. How did the boys feel once they had been transported to the room by the genie?

_____

More things to do → Write down what you think Kirpal's next command to the genie will be.

Continued from P40

A narrow escape

An adventure story is a type of narrative. At the start we are introduced to the characters and find out what the adventure will be. This introduction is followed by exciting happenings and an ending in which everything is worked out.

Before you read ➤ Think of some places where an adventure story called 'A narrow escape' might take place.

Read this story ➤

A NARROW ESCAPE

Lucy heard the order above the boom of the cascading water: "Paddles in. Lean left."

She obeyed, as if by instinct, and the rubber raft surged down the rapid, through the gap in the rocks, and moved swiftly into calmer, safer water. Another crisis was over.

"Are you OK, Lucy?"

That was her father.

"Paddle hard, left. Now!"

That was the instructor.

Lucy paddled furiously, hardly drawing breath. She tried to feel brave by remembering that the instructor knew the river like the back of his hand.

"The toughest stretch is round the next bend, crew!" he yelled. "Do exactly as I say and we'll make it all right. Lucy, sit next to me and hang on tight to the rope. Good luck everyone!"

The raft started to gather speed. Lucy could see the frothy rapids ahead. She was scared – really scared. Crash! The raft bounced off the rocky wall of the cliff on the right. Thump! It landed hard, after plunging down a steep cascade of water. Still the little crew clung on and the raft rushed forward, swept faster and faster and faster by the surging water. Just when she thought that the nightmare would go on forever she heard the instructor shout, "One more drop, crew, a big one, and then we're through."

The raft's nose turned downwards and plunged over the waterfall. It hit the bottom hard and nearly turned over. Lucy's grip on the rope loosened; almost as if in slow motion she felt herself tip; and then she was in the raging water!

There was silence all around her, the silence of the deep. Her lungs wanted air, but she knew she had to hold her breath. Up,

Continued on P43

■SCHOLASTIC **Photocopiable**

up through the bubbles she went. And then, just as her lungs felt like they were about to burst, she broke the surface and gasped air – beautiful air.

Then she felt something grab her life jacket and lift her, dripping, out of the water. It was the strong arm of the instructor.

"Got you, young tadpole," he said, as he pulled Lucy on board. Welcome to the club, the Tadpole Club. Only rafters who fall over the side are allowed to join. It's very exclusive."

Lucy saw her father's grey, worried face and smiled at him. "I'm OK, Dad," she gasped. "I'm just a very wet tadpole."

Re-read the story   **Answer the following questions.**

1. Which character was an experienced rafter? _____

_____

2. What was the raft made of? _____

3. Why do you think the instructor asked Lucy to sit by him? _____

_____

_____

4. Why did Lucy's father look grey and worried? _____

_____

5. How did a rafter become a member of the Tadpole Club? _____

_____

6. Why do you think it was called the Tadpole Club? _____

_____

_____

7. What is the crisis (the most tense and exciting moment) in this story? _____

_____

Continued from P42

Trouble at home

A play usually involves two or more characters talking to each other. This is called dialogue. A play often has some suggestions about where the scene is taking place and what the characters are doing. These are stage directions.

Before you read

- From the title of the play, what do you expect it to be about?
- Have you seen, heard or read any plays? What were they called?
- Are some radio and television commercials short plays? Why do you think so?

Read this play

TROUBLE AT HOME

Joshua and Luke are on the school bus on their way home. Joshua is a bit worried because his dad has just lost his job.

JOSHUA: I don't know what Dad's goin' to do. He's lost his job. Company went broke.

LUKE: Went broke? So they let him go?

JOSHUA: Yeah. I don't think it's fair.

LUKE: What did he do?

JOSHUA: Drove a truck.

LUKE: It's bad luck! What's he goin' to do?

JOSHUA: Look for a job. He checks the paper every mornin'.

LUKE: Hasn't found anything?

JOSHUA: Naw! Rung up for a couple of jobs but didn't get 'em. (He *pauses as if he is thinking of something. He frowns*) He gets grumpy about it.

LUKE: That's what happened to my dad. When he lost his job, him and mum started fightin'.

JOSHUA: Yeah I know.

LUKE: He went for a job today. A mate of his told him about it. I've got my fingers crossed.

JOSHUA: I hope my dad finds a job soon.

LUKE: Yeah, it's rotten. Got to get off next stop. Hope your dad finds somethin' soon.

JOSHUA: Me too. See ya.

Continued on P45

SCHOLASTIC **Photocopiable**

Re-read the play ➤ **Answer the following questions.**
(Use the back of the sheet for question 11.)

1. Who are the two characters in the play? _____

_____

2. Whose father has just lost his job? _____

3. What does Joshua's father do each morning? _____

_____

4. Where is Luke's father going today? _____

_____

5. How do you know that Joshua is feeling worried? _____

_____

6. At what time of day is the conversation between Joshua and Luke taking place?

_____

7. Why do you think the play is called 'Trouble at home'? _____

_____

8. What does **Company went broke** mean? _____

_____

9. What problems might be caused for a family if a parent lost his or her job?

_____

_____

10. How do people go about looking for new jobs? _____

_____

11. What do you notice about this play that makes it different from an ordinary story?

Continued from P44 ➤

 **Photocopiable**

The Hare and the Tortoise

In a play the characters are given lines to say to each other (or to themselves). When characters talk to each other this is called dialogue. Plays are usually acted on a stage, and the place where the action happens is called the scene. Instructions on how the stage should look and what the actors should do are called stage directions (they are often in italic writing).

Before you read

Have you heard this story before? Can you remember who won the race?

Read this play

THE HARE AND THE TORTOISE

Hare is boasting to Tortoise about how fast he can run. They are in a woodland setting with a winning post at the back.

HARE: You are the slowest thing I've ever seen, Tortoise. Anyone could beat you in a race.

TORTOISE: I am slow, Hare, but you shouldn't be so sure of beating me. I never give up.

HARE: (*in a scornful tone*) Tortoise, you are so slow you couldn't beat time. (*Laughing at his own joke*) Ha, ha, ha, ha!

TORTOISE: I might be slow, but I can tell you, I'm steady.

HARE: You could never beat me, Tortoise. No one has ever beaten me. Ever!

TORTOISE: (*in a slow and steady voice*) I… could… beat… you… Hare.

HARE: We'll see about that, old slow coach. I challenge you to a race.

TORTOISE: And I accept the challenge.

HARE: Ready, get set, go!

(*Hare runs so fast he is soon out of sight of Tortoise. He stops, scratches himself and yawns.*)

HARE: (*to himself*) Ho, hum! This is so boring, I think I'll take a nap. Ho, hum! Zzzzzzzzzzzz…

TORTOISE: (*comes along behind and sees* HARE *sleeping*) Well, look at that! I've just passed Hare! And I can see the finishing line ahead!

Continued on P47

HARE: (*wakes suddenly*) What! Where am I? Oh dear! Oh the race! I've got to get to the finishing line!

TORTOISE: (*crosses the line ahead of* HARE) Too late, boaster. I've won! Remember in future: slow and steady wins the race.

AUDIENCE: (*cheering*) Hooray for Tortoise!

Re-read the play

Answer the following questions.
(Use the back of the sheet for questions 7 to 9.)

1. Who are the two main characters? _____

_____

2. What did Hare do that made him lose the race? _____

_____

3. What message did Tortoise give Hare in the end? _____

_____

4. What did Hare say that showed he was boastful? _____

_____

_____

5. Who did the audience like better – Hare or Tortoise? Explain why. _____

_____

_____

6. Here are some words that describe the two characters in this play. These words are adjectives. Circle the adjectives that suit Hare in one colour and those that fit Tortoise in another.

steady   boastful   overconfident   scornful   fast   patient

impatient   determined   persistent   wise   rude   slow

7. If you were Hare, what would you have done?
8. Do you think Hare will remember Tortoise's advice?
9. Do you think **slow and steady** is always enough to win races?

Continued from P46

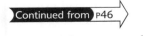

The haunted house

This piece of drama has been written as a radio play. When you listen to a radio play you must use your imagination because you cannot see what is happening. Sound effects are important, and the characters' voices must be very expressive.

Before you read

What sounds might you hear in a haunted house?

Read this radio play

THE HAUNTED HOUSE

Night sounds – the hoot of an owl, the croak of a frog, the howl of a dog in the distance. Footsteps are heard. Two girls are approaching an old house.

JOANNE: (*in a shaking voice*) I'm scared, Tanya. Let's go home.

TANYA: (*in a much firmer voice*) Don't be a wimp, Joanne. You're not still worrying about ghosts, are you? There are no such things as ghosts. Here's the place. Let me switch the torch on. (A *click is heard.*) Does the light make you feel better?

JOANNE: (*still shaky and uncertain*) But we should be at your house. My Mum will be mad if she knows we're here.

TANYA: Oh, stop fussing! Our houses are only over the road. We can soon run back. It's an adventure.

JOANNE: I don't like adventures. This place has been empty for years. It could be dangerous, and I've heard people say that it's haunted.

(*More night sounds are heard and the moaning of the wind.*)

TANYA: Look! The back door's open. Let's go in.

(*There is a creaking sound as the door is opened wider, then the shuffling sound of the girls' footsteps as they go inside.*)

TANYA: (*in a firm whisper*) There's nothing in here to be scared of. Nothing at all, apart from an old couch.

(A *spooky, rustling sound is heard – crumpled paper can be used.*)

JOANNE: (*terrified*) Listen to that noise! What is it? It's coming from the other room. It must be the ghost!

TANYA: (*now frightened too*) And it's coming closer! Quick – behind the couch!

Continued on P49

(*A thump and a bump are heard as the girls dive behind the couch.*)

TANYA: I'll turn off the torch. (*A click is heard.*) Lie still!

JOANNE: (*in a panic*) It's the ghost. It's coming to get us!

(*The rustling sound becomes louder. The girls scream.*)

TANYA: I've got to see what it is.

(*A click is heard as the torch is turned on, then a pause,
then the meow of a lonely cat.*)

JOANNE: (*relieved*) Look Tanya – it's a cat! Only a cat.

TANYA: (*firmly*) There's your ghost, Joanne. A poor hungry cat.
Let's take it home.

(*The cat meows again.*)

TANYA: (*patting the cat*) Come on, nice Ghostie. We'll give you
some milk.

(*The cat begins to purr. Night sounds are heard again,
but softer and less threatening in the background.*)

Re-read the radio play

Answer the following questions.
(Use the back of the sheet for questions 4 t0 7.)

1. At what time of day do you think the play took place? _____

_____

2. What did the girls do when they heard the ghostly sound? _____

_____

3. Which girl was braver? Give your reasons. _____

_____

_____

4. ● Why do the girls go into the haunted house?
    ● Would you have gone in?
5. Why are the sound effects very important in this play?
6. This play has a surprise ending. What is it?
7. What words tell you that the girls were frightened?

Continued from P48

First day in Year 3

A recount tells about an experience that happened in the past. This is a recount of what happened during someone's first day in Year 3.

Before you read

- Think of two things you remember about your first day in Year 3.
- Name two children or adults you remember clearly from your first day in Year 3.
- What was your happiest experience on your first day in Year 3?

Read this recount

FIRST DAY IN YEAR 3

On Tuesday I went into Year 3. It was my first day in the Big School. Our class had some new children but most of them came up from Year 2. I knew them pretty well. I sat next to my friend, Ben. The new children had no friends. I felt sorry for them.

My new teacher was called Mr Rigg. He is quite young and really friendly. I found it hard to call him Mr Rigg. It was the first time I'd had a man teacher.

Our classroom looked a bit bare on the first day. There were so many things around the walls when we were in Year 2. Maybe all of last year's Year 3 had taken their work home. We will need to smarten our room up. I'll tell Mr Rigg. He won't mind.

The Big School was more strict than the Infants. Everyone seemed to be lining up all the time and you were not allowed to walk around the classroom much.

In the morning on our first day in Year 3, we did some writing. I wrote a story about our camping holiday. Ben didn't go away during his holiday, but he made up a story about a terrifying face-to-face meeting with a big snake. In his story he stared hard at the snake until it slithered away. In real life Ben would have run a mile! He's no hero, I can tell you.

In the afternoon Mr Rigg read us a great story about a haunted house. He made it sound really scary! I think I'm going to like Year 3.

Continued on P51

SCHOLASTIC Photocopiable

Re-read the recount ➤ **Answer the following questions.**

1. What was the name of the writer's friend? _____

_____

2. What was the name of the new teacher? _____

_____

3. ● What happened in the morning? _____

   ● What happened in the afternoon? _____

4. What did Ben write about? _____

_____

5. Why did the writer find it hard to call the teacher Mr Rigg? _____

_____

6. Which classroom had more things around the walls, Year 2 or Year 3? _____

_____

7. What things made the writer happy on the first day in Year 3? _____

_____

_____

8. What are the bad things about being new in a class or school? _____

_____

_____

9. What does the writer mean by **He's no hero, I can tell you**? _____

_____

More things to do ➤ Write a recount of your first day in Year 3, or your first day in any new school or class that you remember well.

Continued from P50

A letter to Grandma

Letters can do many different jobs. This letter is to a grandmother, telling her about a flight to the Channel Islands. It is a recount, so it starts off by giving her basic information on when and where the flight took place. It then tells her more about the flight.

Before you read

- For what other reasons might you write to your grandmother?
- Imagine that you are going to take a flight to the Channel Islands. What things might you think about during the flight?
- Why would you and your family go to the Channel Islands?

Read this letter

> Seaview Guest House
> St Helier
> Jersey
>
> Wednesday
>
> Dear Grandma,
>
> We caught the 10am flight to the Channel Islands on Sunday. It left Manchester on time and took just over an hour to get here.
>
> As we taxied to the end of the runway, the flight attendant told us a few things about the plane. She also showed us the exits.
>
> The pilot told us to make sure our seat belts were fastened. Then he revved the engines and we began to race down the runway. It was great! The plane went faster and faster and I felt as if I was being pushed back into the seat. Then all of a sudden we were off the ground. Everything looked smaller and smaller as we went up.
>
> We went into a cloud and the plane started to bump. I closed my eyes. Dad and Mum closed their eyes too. I think they were a bit scared.
>
> We were given a sandwich and a biscuit, and I had a glass of lemonade. By the time the flight attendant had collected up the rubbish, the plane was coming in to land on Jersey. I could feel the plane descending in the sky and the pilot gave us a smooth landing. The engines make a lot of noise when a plane is landing!
>
> When we climbed out of the plane, it was much warmer. Then I knew we were really on our holiday.
>
> Mum and Dad send their love. Me too,
>
> Stephanie

Continued on P53

Re-read the letter

Answer the following questions.
(Use the back of the sheet for question 11.)

1. From what part of the Channel Islands was the letter sent? _____

_____

2. When did the flight leave Manchester? Was it morning or night? _____

_____

3. Who told the passengers about the plane? _____

_____

4. What did Stephanie drink during the flight? _____

_____

5. What made the plane bump about? _____

_____

6. Why did Stephanie think her parents were frightened? _____

_____

7. Do you think Stephanie was a bit frightened too? _____

_____

8. Do you think Stephanie had ever flown before? _____

_____

9. Do you think she enjoyed the flight? _____

_____

10. What do you think is meant by these words?

revved _____

descending _____

11. What would you like about a plane journey?

Continued from P52

A letter to a school friend

A recount tells you about an experience that happened in the past. This letter is a recount. Look closely at how it is set out.

Before you read

- At what time of year do people go skiing?
- Think of two reasons why a person who is on a skiing holiday might write to his or her school friends.

Read this letter

Alphorn Chalet
Rue St Antoine
Beauville
Switzerland

19 January

Dear Abigail,

Disaster today – it is too windy to ski! Last night there was a blizzard, which is still raging. As I look through my window, all I can see is snow blowing everywhere. Everyone is staying indoors.

Up until yesterday the weather was perfect for skiing. Oliver and I have had skiing lessons every morning. Even Mum and Dad go to a ski class. The teachers are all very young and are great skiers. They show you what to do and then give you a chance to try. It looks easy but is often very hard work. My ski instructor says I am learning very quickly.

After our lesson we spend a couple of hours skiing down the slopes. Dad and Mum are good skiers, so they can do the hard runs. Oliver and I just ski down the gentle slopes. We find that's hard enough for us. We still fall over a lot!

Skiing makes you very hungry, so we always have a huge lunch when we get back to the chalet.

I hope this blizzard blows out today so we can ski again tomorrow. If it's fine, the snow will be great.

See you next week back at school.

Love Danielle

Continued on P55

Re-read the letter

Answer the following questions.
(Use the back of the sheet for questions 10 and 11.)

1. Where was Danielle staying on her skiing holiday? _____

_____

2. Who is on holiday with Danielle? _____

_____

3. Why was Danielle writing to her friend, Abigail, today? _____

_____

4. Where did Danielle normally eat lunch while she was on holiday? _____

_____

5. Why did Danielle and Oliver take skiing lessons? _____

_____

6. Why did Danielle's mother and father take skiing lessons if they were already good skiers?

_____

7. Do you think Danielle was enjoying her holiday? What makes you think this?

_____

_____

8. What is a chalet? _____

_____

9. What is a blizzard? _____

_____

10. Name some countries in which people go skiing.

11. Imagine you are skiing down a snow-covered mountain. Write down three things that you might see.

Continued from P54

SCHOLASTIC **Photocopiable**

Scrambled eggs on toast

A recipe is one form of instruction. It tells you what you need and gives you step-by-step instructions on how to prepare the dish.

Before you read

- Would you prepare scrambled eggs for breakfast, lunch or tea? Why?
- Who might you cook scrambled eggs for?
- What ingredients and kitchen tools might you use?

Read this recipe

SCRAMBLED EGGS ON TOAST
(SERVES 2)

Ingredients
4 fresh eggs
butter or margarine
finely chopped parsley
milk
salt
bread

You will need
whisk or fork
mixing bowl
medium-sized saucepan
sharp kitchen knife
wooden spoon
chopping board
toaster

Method
1. Break eggs into bowl and beat well.
2. Add small amount of milk and pinch of salt.
3. Beat again until well mixed.
4. Melt small amount of butter or margarine in pan.
5. Pour egg mixture into pan.
6. Cook until egg is no longer runny, stirring constantly with wooden spoon.
7. Toast and butter one or two slices of bread per person.
8. Spoon egg onto toast.
9. Sprinkle with parsley.

Continued on p57

Re-read the recipe → **Answer the following questions.**

1. How many eggs do you need for this recipe? _____

2. What would you use to beat the eggs? _____

_____

3. What type of pan would you use? _____

_____

4. What other method of cooking food is mentioned in the recipe? _____

_____

5. Why do you think you use butter or margarine in the pan? _____

_____

6. Why would you sprinkle parsley on the scrambled eggs? _____

_____

7. How many eggs would you need to feed four people? _____

_____

8. Scrambled eggs are often considered suitable food for young children or people who are ill. Why might this be?

_____

9. Name at least three other ways of cooking food. _____

_____

10. Here is a set of commands for cleaning your teeth correctly. Number them in the correct order.

Rinse out mouth and rinse toothbrush. ☐

Squeeze toothpaste onto toothbrush. ☐

Brush teeth up and down. Don't forget gums. ☐

Continued from p56 >

Tug of war

An instruction tells you how something is done. Rules for games are instructions. These rules tell you how many players there are, what you need to play the game and the steps you must follow.

Before you read

- What is your favourite game?
- Name one thing you need in order to play it.
- Think of two things you have to do when you play it.

Read these instructions

TUG OF WAR

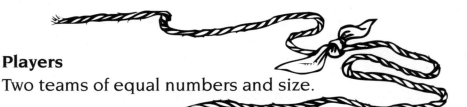

Players
Two teams of equal numbers and size.

Materials
(what you need)
Long, thick rope (with a piece of cloth tied at the halfway mark).
Line on the ground.

Steps
(what to do)
1. Line teams up facing each other.
2. Tell teams to hold rope.
3. Give order, "Pull!"
4. Declare winner when one team pulls the other over line marked on the ground.

Continued on p59

Re-read the instructions

Answer the following questions.
(Use the back of the sheet for question 10.)

1. What is the aim of these instructions? _____

_____

2. Name two things you need for a tug of war. _____

_____

3. How many players are needed to play the game? _____

_____

4. How does a team know when to start? _____

_____

5. What does a team need to do to win? _____

_____

6. Why do you think the teams should be of equal number and size? _____

_____

7. Why does the rope need to be thick? _____

_____

8. What sort of people would you like to have on your team in a tug of war? _____

_____

9. Have you ever run in a book race (where you race with a book on your head!)?
Here are the steps for that race. Number them in the correct order.

Tell runners who drop book to go back to start.   ☐

Begin race.   ☐

Give prize to runner who is first over line with book on head.   ☐

Line up runners, each with book on head.   ☐

10. Tug of war is a team game. Write the names of at least two other team games.

Continued from p58

How to plant a tree

An instruction tells you how something is done. You have to know what you need and the steps you must follow.

Before you read ▶ If you have planted, or helped to plant, a tree at home or at school, think of two things you did which were very important. If you have not planted a tree, what things do you think might be important?

Read these instructions ▶

HOW TO PLANT A TREE

Materials
(what you need)
tree in pot or other container
spade
watering can
fertiliser or compost (if available)
small stake
tree tie

Tree in pot

Steps
(what to do)
1. Dig hole (larger than container) in ground.
2. Loosen soil in hole.
3. Water hole and allow water to soak in.
4. Turn tree container upside down.
5. Hold tree and remove from pot with care.
6. Place tree in hole.
7. Pack earth firmly around roots.
8. Spread compost or fertiliser around tree.
9. Water tree lightly.
10. Push or hammer in stake near tree and fix with tree tie.

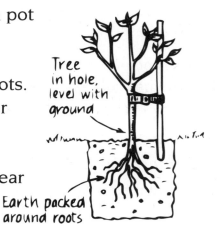

Tree in hole, level with ground

Earth packed around roots

Continued on ▶ p61

SCHOLASTIC Photocopiable

Re-read the instructions ➤ **Answer the following questions.**

1. Name three things you need to plant a tree. _____

_____

2. Name three things you do when you are planting a tree. _____

_____

3. Why do you need water? _____

4. What is the spade used for? _____

5. Why would the hole need to be larger than the pot? _____

_____

_____

6. Why might you need to pack the earth tightly around the roots? _____

_____

7. Do you know what a stake is? What would it be used for? _____

_____

8. What are compost and fertiliser? _____

_____

9. These instructions on how to plant a tree are laid out in steps. The steps are numbered 1 to 10. How does this help the reader?

_____

_____

10. The diagrams with the instructions are labelled. How do the labels help the reader?

_____

_____

Continued from p60 ➤

Football

A report is organised into two parts: a statement of what the report is about, and facts about the subject.

Before you read

- How popular a sport is football?
- Does each player have a special job in a football team? What position do you play or would like to play?
- Why do you think so many people like football?

Read this report

FOOTBALL

Football, or soccer, is one of the most popular games around the world. It is played on a field that has goalposts at either end. There is a net behind the goalposts. This net catches the ball when it goes into the goal. The ball is round and is inflated with air.

There are two teams of eleven players. A team scores a goal when one of its players kicks the football into the net. This would be easier if there were no goalkeeper or goalie. The goalie's job is to stop the ball going over the goal line between the posts. He is the only player who is allowed to touch the ball with his hands. All the others have to play it with their feet or their heads, except when throwing it in after it has gone out of play.

Every player in the team has a job to do. The goalkeeper stops the ball going into his goal with the help of his defenders. Midfield players help the defenders and pass the ball to the forwards. The forwards' job is to score goals.

Football is played by boys and girls, men and women all over the world. It is an Olympic sport. The most famous football event in the world is the World Cup. When teams play, many millions of people watch the matches on television.

Continued on P63

Re-read the report

Answer the following questions.
(Use the back of the sheet for question 10.)

1. What is another name for football? _____

2. Where is a net used in football? _____

3. Is football played by both girls and boys? _____

4. What is the most famous football event in the world? _____

_____

5. Why is it difficult to score a goal? _____

_____

6. Why is the goalkeeper the only person who can handle the ball? _____

_____

_____

7. Why do so many girls and boys enjoy playing football? _____

_____

_____

8. Why is football watched by more people on television than any other sport? _____

_____

9. What does **Olympic sport** mean? _____

_____

10. This report uses special football language. Write down the meanings of these words or phrases.

inflated with air   net   goalkeeper   forward   defend

More things to do

- Find out the names of all the players in your local football team (or another team of your choice).
- Find out the names of two famous clubs from other countries.

Continued from P62

The fairy penguin

A report provides us with facts (information) about something. It begins with an opening statement and then gives us a number of different facts.

Before you read →

- Do you think a penguin is a:
  ...fish? ...bird? ...mammal?

- Which of these is true?
  Penguins can fly.
  Penguins can swim and walk.

Read this report →

THE FAIRY PENGUIN

Fairy penguins are the smallest type of penguin in the world. They live in the south of Australia and in New Zealand.

Fairy penguins weigh about 1 kilogram and stand 30 centimetres high. Their back feathers are dark blue and their front feathers are white. They have a beak, webbed feet and flippers.

Penguins live on the land and in the sea. They are very good swimmers and divers, but they cannot fly. They eat small fish and squid.

Fairy penguins breed on land. The female lays two white eggs in a burrow, and the male and female share the job of sitting on the eggs. When the babies hatch they are covered in white down.

At the start the mother and father bring food from the sea, but after eight weeks the baby penguins have grown feathers and are soon ready to hunt for their own food.

Fairy penguins are often in danger. They are hunted by wild animals; they are caught in nets and on long lines; if they get covered with oil, they drown. Many of their breeding grounds have been taken over by humans who have gone to live there. If their numbers become too small, these little penguins might disappear for ever.

Continued on P65 →

■SCHOLASTIC **Photocopiable**

Re-read the report ➤   **Answer the following questions.**

1. What are the smallest penguins in the world? _____

   _____

2. Where do they live? _____

3. What colour is the back of a fairy penguin? _____

4. What do fairy penguins eat? _____

5. Why would webbed feet be important for fairy penguins? _____

   _____

6. How do you think these penguins catch their food? _____

   _____

7. Why might an oil tanker sinking cause danger to fairy penguins? _____

   _____

   _____

8. Do you think that fairy penguins should be protected? _____

   _____

9. What do you think we should do to protect fairy penguins? _____

   _____

10. What do you think **breeding grounds** are? _____

    _____

11. Complete these sentences.

Penguins _____ on the land and in the sea.

The females _____ two white eggs in a burrow.

The chicks are soon ready to _____ for their own food.

Continued from P64 ➤

Learning to swim

A factual report begins with a statement of what the report is about and then gives some facts about the subject.

Before you read

- Can you swim? How did you learn? Who taught you how to swim?
- Which of these did you find hardest when you were learning to swim?
    Putting your head under water.
    Learning to kick your legs.
    Learning to move your arms and kick your legs at the same time.

Read this report

LEARNING TO SWIM

Many children learn to swim when they are quite young. Sometimes they learn during the school holidays at special classes held at local swimming pools. The teachers have special training so they can teach young children water safety and how to swim.

Young children start to learn how to do simple things like putting their heads under water. Often this is at the shallow end of a pool, but even here some very small children may not be able to touch the bottom. If not, they can always hold on to the edge of the pool and learn how to kick their legs.

Most children learn swimming strokes after just a few lessons but often when they start they can only do a type of doggy paddle. It is most important that as they get older and stronger they should take some more lessons. In this way they will become good and strong swimmers and will also learn about how to behave sensibly in the water.

Learning to swim is important, but learning to swim *well* is just as important.

Continued on P67

Answer the following questions.
(Use the back of the sheet for questions 10 and 11.)

1. When do many children learn to swim? _____

_____

2. When and where are the special swimming classes held? _____

_____

3. At which end of the pool do children often start learning to swim? _____

_____

4. What do you need to do in order to become a good, strong swimmer? _____

_____

5. Why are children taught to put their heads under water? _____

_____

6. Why is shallow water more suitable for new swimmers? _____

_____

7. What do you think **doggy paddle** is? _____

_____

8. Who swims at the deep end? _____

_____

9. Give at least one reason why it is important to learn how to swim. _____

_____

_____

10. List what you think are the differences between learning to swim and learning
to swim really well.

11. What sort of training do you think is needed in order to teach swimming?

Continued from P66

Why the sea is salty

An explanation makes clear how things work or why things happen. It opens with a general statement and then lists points which explain how or why.

Before you read

- Which is more salty, water from a tap or water in the sea?
- Where do rivers run to?

Read this explanation

WHY THE SEA IS SALTY

The sea is salty because salt is washed into the sea from the land.

First, rain washes salt from the ground, and this salt dissolves in the rainwater before running into the rivers. When the rivers flow into the sea they carry the salt with them.

Every year millions of tonnes of salt are washed into the sea, and when water evaporates from the sea, the salt is left behind. This means that the sea contains more and more salt as the years go by.

The Red Sea and the Dead Sea are more salty than the oceans. This is because they have many rivers flowing into them. Also, they are inland seas and not very big, so the salt builds up. The extra salt in the water makes it very easy to swim in these seas.

The rain washes out the salt from the land

Salty water goes into the rivers

The rivers flow into the sea with the salt

Continued on P69

 SCHOLASTIC Photocopiable

Re-read the explanation ➤ **Answer the following questions.**

1. Does salt dissolve in water? _____

2. What carries the salt to the sea? _____

   _____

3. How much salt is washed into the sea each year? _____

   _____

4. Which seas are easy to swim in? _____

   _____

5. Is the Red Sea more salty than the Atlantic Ocean? _____

   _____

6. Will the sea become more salty as time goes by? Why? _____

   _____

7. What else do you think rivers carry to the sea besides salt? _____

   _____

   _____

8. What other things dissolve in water? _____

   _____

9. What do you think it would be like to swim in the Dead Sea? _____

   _____

10. Write **true** or **false** after these sentences.

When water evaporates from the sea, salt is left behind. _____

The oceans are more salty than the Red Sea or the Dead Sea. _____

Salt is carried into the sea by rivers that flow into the sea. _____

Continued from P68 ➤

SCHOLASTIC **Photocopiable**

How to find information in a book

An explanation helps the reader to understand why things are done or how they work. It begins with a general statement and then presents reasons.

Before you read

- How do you go about finding information in a book?
- Where would you find lots of books in a school?

Read this explanation

HOW TO FIND INFORMATION IN A BOOK

Books often contain a lot of information. It can be a great help to us if we know how to find the information we need quickly.

All books have a title, which acts as the first clue. For example, if the title of a book is *Famous Steam Trains*, we know immediately that the book will have information on steam trains.

The title of a book and the name of the author are printed on the cover and on the title page.

Most books have a contents page. This lists all the different sections in the book. So, in the example *Famous Steam Trains*, the contents page might look something like this:

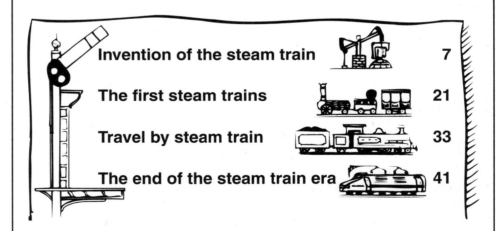

Invention of the steam train	7
The first steam trains	21
Travel by steam train	33
The end of the steam train era	41

Notice that the contents page gives the page number where each section, or chapter, starts. So, if you wanted to find information about travelling by steam train, you would turn to page 33 and read that section. Some books also have an index at the back.

Continued on P71

▪ SCHOLASTIC Photocopiable

Re-read the explanation ➤   **Answer the following questions.**

1. Name two places where the title of the book is printed. _____

_____

2. What does a contents page do? _____

_____

3. Give the name of one section in the book *Famous Steam Trains.* _____

_____

4. On what page would **The end of the steam train era** begin? _____

_____

5. What other name is often used for a section in a book? _____

_____

6. Why might you need to be able to find information in a book quickly? _____

_____

7. Do you think a contents page would be helpful for this? Why? _____

_____

8. What information would you find on a title page? _____

_____

9. Mark whether these sentences are **true** or **false**.

All books have an index at the back. _____

Most books have a contents page. _____

The name of the author is always on the back cover. _____

You need to use the title page to find out where each chapter begins. _____

The book *Famous Steam Trains* has four chapters. _____

Continued from P70 ➤

Why there is lightning then thunder

An explanation makes clear how things work or why things happen. It opens with an overall statement followed by points which explain how or why.

Before you read →

When you see lightning, what do you usually hear?

Read this explanation →

WHY THERE IS LIGHTNING THEN THUNDER

Thunderstorms are the most common type of storm. They happen when warm, damp air rises and then forms clouds as it cools. Thunderclouds are huge and black, and they stretch very high into the sky. The currents of air inside the cloud cause heavy rain, thunder and lightning.

Lightning is really a giant electric spark, which is often several kilometres long. Thunder is the noise made when the lightning causes the air to heat up and expand suddenly. When this explodes we hear the sound we call thunder.

A lightning flash, and the clap of thunder that comes from it, happen at about the same time. We see the lightning first and hear the thunder later because light travels very quickly and we see it almost immediately. Sound travels much more slowly and so takes longer to reach our ears. If the lightning is several kilometres away this may take a number of seconds.

One way to tell if a flash of lightning is a long way off is to count the seconds until you hear the thunder. If you count three seconds, then the lightning and thunder are about one kilometre off. If the flash and the thunder seem to happen together, the lightning is very close. Watch out!

Continued on ▶ P73

Re-read the explanation → **Answer the following questions.**
(Use the back of the sheet for questions 7 and 8.)

1. What is lightning? _____

_____

2. What causes thunder? _____

_____

3. Which travels faster – light or sound? _____

_____

4. How can you check if a flash of lightning is a long way off? _____

_____

_____

5. Why would you have to **watch out** if the flash of lightning and the sound of thunder seemed to occur together?

_____

_____

6. Why is it not dangerous if you hear thunder long after you see the flash of lightning?

_____

_____

7. What should you do to be safe from lightning if you are caught out in a storm?
8. Thunderstorms are just one kind of storm. Can you think of any others?
9. Mark these sentences **true** or **false**.

Lightning and thunder never occur simultaneously. _____

If you count 15 seconds in between thunder and lightning, the storm is about 5

kilometres away. _____

Thunder is the sound of warm air colliding with cool air. _____

Continued from P72 →

We should look after our trees

An argument gives a particular view about something and the information that supports this view. At the end it sums up all the points that have been made.

Before you read

- What are two things you like about trees?
- Do you know the name of a type of tree that you see near your house or school?
- Think of one reason why trees are important to birds and animals.

Read this argument

WE SHOULD LOOK AFTER OUR TREES

We should always remember to look after our trees as they are very important for our planet and in our lives.

First, trees keep the air pure because they give off the gas oxygen, which humans and animals need to breathe. They also take in other gases, like carbon dioxide, that we do not need.

Second, because the roots of trees hold the soil together they stop it from being washed away. In some parts of the world where a great many trees have been cut down, the land has been completely destroyed.

Trees provide homes for many different types of birds and animals, and they also supply their food. If trees are cut down, there will be no place for these birds and animals to live and nothing for them to eat.

In addition, trees often help in keeping us cool because they shade us from the hot sun. Sometimes they also offer shelter or protection from bad weather.

Finally, trees are beautiful to look at. The world would be a much uglier place if there were no trees.

All around the world forests are being cut down. We should look after the trees that are left and make sure that more are planted to replace those that have already been destroyed.

Continued on P75

SCHOLASTIC Photocopiable

Re-read the argument

Answer the following questions.
(Use the back of the sheet for question 7.)

1. Write five reasons why we should look after our trees. Use your own words.

_____

_____

_____

_____

2. Why are trees important to animals and birds? _____

_____

3. Why might trees be very important in summer? _____

_____

4. What parts of trees do you think birds and animals eat? _____

_____

_____

5. Write a sentence which sums up the argument. _____

_____

_____

6. Number these statements in the order in which they appear in the argument.

Trees keep us cool because they shade us from the hot sun. ☐

Trees are beautiful to look at. ☐

Trees keep the air pure as they give off oxygen and take in carbon dioxide. ☐

Trees provide homes for birds and animals. ☐

The roots of trees hold the soil together. ☐

7. Imagine a world without trees. Can you list some bad things about it?

Continued from P74

Going to school

An argument begins with the author stating a point of view. This is followed by reasons that support that point of view. The author ends by summing up and coming to a conclusion.

Before you read ➤

- Why do you go to school? Give three reasons.
- What do you think is the most important thing you learn at school?
- Name some other places where you learn things.

Read this argument ➤

GOING TO SCHOOL

Going to school is very important because during the years that we are at school we learn many things. By law, all children in the UK between the ages of five and sixteen must attend a school and be taught, or educated, in many subjects.

As very young children we learn to read and write. These are sometimes called literacy skills. We also learn to work with numbers (sometimes called numeracy). It is important to learn these skills. We need them for all kinds of things in life as we grow up, not only for things we do at school.

At school we are also taught a great deal about our world and the people who live in it. By understanding other countries and other peoples we should be able to make our world a better place to live.

While we are at school we learn to work together and to help each other. This helps us to understand and appreciate what we can do best and also what others can do well.

Good health and fitness often begin with sports played at school which we enjoy, but which also help us to become fit and well. As being fit is important all our lives it is a good thing to recognise this at an early age.

At school we learn a lot of different things. Many of these will be of help to us all through our lives.

Continued on ▶P77

■ SCHOLASTIC Photocopiable

Re-read the argument

Answer the following questions.
(Use the back of the sheet for questions 8 to 11.)

1. At what age must children in the UK start school? _____

_____

2. For how many years must UK children attend school? _____

_____

3. Name three things we learn about when we first go to school. _____

_____

4. Complete the following sentences.

Reading and writing are sometimes called _____ skills.

Another word for learning to work with numbers is _____ .

5. Do we use these skills only while we are at school? _____

_____

6. Why is it important to learn these things? _____

_____

7. What does playing sport at school teach us? _____

_____

8. How might we make our world a better place to live by knowing about other countries and the people who live in them?

9. In team sports we develop health and fitness and which other important skill mentioned?

10. What other things, not mentioned in the article, do you think are important lessons that are learned at school?

11. For what jobs, as adults, might we be glad of the numeracy skills we learn at school?

More things to do

Write an argument in which the main idea is one of your own choice.

Continued from P76

Things were better then

An argument presents a particular view about something and then gives points that support this view. It sums the view up at the end.

Before you read ➤ Do you think that life was better for boys and girls when Grandpa and Grandma were young? Give one reason for your view.

Read this argument ➤

THINGS WERE BETTER THEN

I think that boys and girls had a better life when Grandpa and Grandma were young.

First, cities and towns were not so crowded then. It would have been easier to get about and find space to play.

Second, the air was much cleaner than it is today. There were not so many cars, lorries, planes or factories causing pollution.

Our rivers and oceans were clean, too. There was not much rubbish, industrial waste or algae in them.

As there were very few cars, boys and girls could ride their bikes in safety. There was also less crime, which meant that parents didn't have to worry so much about their children being in danger.

Lastly, there was much more opportunity for boys and girls to spend time outdoors. Nowadays more and more trees are being cut down to build more and more houses, but then, even in the cities, there were more grassy areas with room for everyone to play.

All of these things make me think that life was better for boys and girls in my grandparents' day.

Continued on ▶ P79

Re-read the argument

Answer the following questions.
(Use the back of the sheet for questions 9 and 10.)

1. Were there more, or fewer, people living in cities in our grandparents' day?

_____

2. In what way was the air different then? _____

_____

3. Why was this? _____

_____

4. Do boys and girls spend more, or less, time outdoors nowadays? _____

_____

5. Why can't you ride your bike anywhere you wish today? _____

_____

6. Find one sentence which sums up the argument. _____

_____

7. How do cars, lorries, planes and factories cause pollution? _____

_____

_____

8. How do our rivers and oceans become polluted? _____

_____

_____

9. Arguments often use special words or phrases called technical terms. Write the meanings of the following three technical terms. Use your dictionary if you need help.

pollution   industrial waste   algae

10. Do you think life was better when Grandpa and Grandma were young? Why?

Continued from P78

Travel teaches you many things

An argument begins with the author stating a point of view. This is followed by reasons that support that point of view. At the end the author sums up the argument to reach a conclusion.

Before you read

Have you ever travelled? Where did you go? Who did you travel with? Why did you travel? What was the most important thing you learned while you were travelling?

Read this argument

TRAVEL TEACHES YOU MANY THINGS

When you travel you are able to learn many things that you cannot learn at school or at home.

By travelling to other countries you can find out about the people who live there. If you are able to spend time in the place where they live you will get a real opportunity to understand many things about the lives of people in other places.

You can see what kind of lifestyles they have – what their homes are like, what they eat, what kind of clothes they wear. You can learn what types of jobs they do, how they get about and how they spend their leisure time. By walking among them, sitting near them in restaurants and buses and hearing the language they speak, you will really start to know them in a way you would never be able to from books, films or television programmes.

You can also learn a lot about yourself. How different is your lifestyle, your language, the food you eat? Could you live like them, eat the food they eat, learn their language? When you start to ask yourself these things, you will learn a great deal about others, and a lot about yourself.

Travel teaches you about other people and other places. It also encourages you to think about yourself and where you live. Many of the things you experience by spending time in another country cannot be learned in any other way.

Continued on P81

SCHOLASTIC Photocopiable

Re-read the argument

Answer the following questions.
(Use the back of the sheet for questions 7 and 8.)

1. Underline the statements that you think are correct.

Travel takes you to where people live.

Travel teaches you about others and yourself.

Travel costs too much so it's not worth it.

You can learn just as much from seeing a programme on TV.

Travel would help nations to understand each other better.

There are too many health risks when you are travelling.

2. List three things you may notice that are different in another country or area.

_____

_____

3. Why is it important to ask questions when you travel? _____

_____

4. What does **lifestyle** mean? _____

_____

5. Do you think you would learn more about yourself, or about other people, if you went travelling?

_____

6. How does the writer sum up this argument? _____

_____

_____

7. Is 'Travel teaches you many things' a good title for this argument? Can you think of a different title that would be suitable?
8. Write down any reasons you can think of that do not support this writer's argument.

Continued from P80

Poetry

1 A Lesson for Young James

Question types: 3 literal; 1 inferential; 1 evaluative; 4 deductive
1. The name of James's first teacher was Mrs King.
2. James was very spoiled when he first came to school.
3. Three words that he used a lot were 'Won't', 'No' and 'Yuk'.
4. James changed because Mrs King wouldn't put up with his behaviour.
5. They must have thought that he was very rude.
6. Own answer.
7. 'lost her cool' – lost her temper; 'Just will not work with me' – will have no effect on me.
8 and 9. Own answers.

2 Grasshoppers

Question types: 4 literal; 2 inferential; 2 evaluative; 1 deductive
1. The poem is about grasshoppers.
2. The insect is green.
3. The poet creeps up on them, then stops.
4. No, the poet has never caught a grasshopper.
5. Their big back legs help them to jump high.
6. The part of the poem that reveals that the poet may be scared of grasshoppers is 'Creeping up/Till they hop?/Or do you stop?'
7. probably young; afraid; timid; interested in creatures.
8. Grasshoppers are wild and green, they have big back legs; The poet is rather timid (he is very careful not to get too close to the grasshoppers), he is interested in grasshoppers and probably other wild creatures.
9. Own answer.

3 See the robbers passing by

Question types: 2 literal; 1 inferential; 2 evaluative; 4 deductive
1. The robber stole a watch and chain.
2. He must go to prison.
3. The words and phrases are 'robbers', 'My fair la-dy!' and 'watch and chain'.
4. A watch would have a chain if it was an old-fashioned pocket watch kept on a chain, rather than one fixed to a strap and worn around the wrist.
5. He would have to be tried and found guilty.
6. Own answer.
7. A highwayman lay in wait for travellers and then robbed them; He rode on horseback.
8. robber – thief; prison – jail.
9. Own answer.

Hare in Summer

Question types: 4 literal; 2 inferential; 1 evaluative; 5 deductive
1. It is summer.
2. The strainer-post is making the shade.
3. The hare changes position to stay in the shade of the post as the sun moves.
4. The hare lifts his 'goggling eyes'.
5. 'weakly panting', 'goggling eyes', 'naked sun'.
6. The third phrase is correct.
7. He is hot and exhausted.
8. He has 'squatted there' to avoid the sun and sit in the shade.
9. Nothing covers the sun; there are no clouds.
10. A 'strainer-post' is a post in the ground to hold another post upright when a wire is tightened.
11. Your skin would start to burn and your body would lose water; if you did not find shade or water you would eventually die.
12. The rhyming words are: 'hare' – 'there'; 'run' – 'sun'; 'shade' – 'made'; 'shifts' – 'lifts'.

Narrative

 The Fox and the Crow

Question types: 5 literal; 2 inferential; 1 evaluative; 1 deductive
1. The crow had found a piece of cheese on the ground.
2. The crow flew on to a branch of a nearby tree.
3. The fox planned to get the cheese by getting the crow to open her mouth.
4. When the crow began to sing the cheese dropped out of her mouth.
5. Don't trust people who flatter you.
6. The fox thought his plan would work because he knew the crow was vain.
7. She was flattered, and was thinking about how the fox thought she could sing well.
8 and 9. Own answers.

 King Midas and the golden touch

Question types: 4 literal; 2 inferential; 2 evaluative; 1 deductive
1. His daughter was called Marigold.
2. The first wish he was granted was that everything he touched would turn to gold; the second wish he was granted was that the golden touch was taken away.
3. He was going to eat pancakes, fresh fruit and an egg.
4. The first problem was that his breakfast turned to gold.
5. The worst thing that happened to him in the story was his daughter turning to gold.
6. He didn't realise that his food and his daughter would turn to gold.
7. Magical things happen that would not occur in real life.
8. 'I have learned my lesson' means that you have realised where you went wrong, and now know not to make that mistake again.
9. Own answer.

7 Katy's dog

Question types: 3 literal; 2 inferential; 1 evaluative; 4 deductive
1. Katy's dog was called Dylan.
2. He had long legs, a short tail and long hair; his coat was a mixture of colours.
3. Two dogs ran at Katy in the park. Dylan stood in their way and fought them off.
4. She trusted him to look after Katy.
5. Usually he barked and ran to her.
6. Answers may vary – Dylan may have chased the dogs and got lost; Her father was right when he said that Dylan would find his way home.
7. He had been fighting and had probably fallen into some mud.
8. A tornado is a fierce and violent storm; Dylan became fierce if Katy was in danger.
9. Katy felt happy and relieved at the end of the story.
10. Own answer.

8 A close shave

Question types: 4 literal; 1 inferential; 1 evaluative; 4 deductive
1. Three people went fishing: the narrator, the narrator's father and Hannah.
2. They put the boat into the water at the slipway.
3. The slipway was on a river.
4. Four fish were caught.
5. The heat and the big, black clouds were the signs that a storm was coming.
6. Own answer.
7. They travelled back in the coastguard launch because their own boat was immobilised; it would be safer.
8. If they hadn't had the mobile phone, they would have been caught in the storm and their boat might have capsized or sunk.
9. Answers may vary – she was probably worried, then relieved, and glad that she had put the mobile phone in the bag.
10. Answers may vary – the story tells about a dangerous situation which could have turned out badly, but didn't.

9 Catherine and the Carrot King

Question types: 5 literal; 2 inferential; 1 evaluative; 1 deductive
1. No, Catherine did not like carrots – raw ones took too long to chew and meant that she didn't get any playtime.
2. The Carrot King had a carrot-coloured coat, a carrot-coloured suit, pointed carrot-coloured shoes and a crown made of carrots.
3. There were dishes of carrots of all kinds – raw and cooked in different ways.
4. The task was that the children had to eat all the carrots by midday.
5. These were the other children who hated carrots.
6. Answers may vary – he may want to persuade them to like carrots because he is king of the carrots or because carrots are good for you.
7. The two main characters are Catherine and the Carrot King.
8. Answers may vary – the reader knows that the passage is a fantasy because of details such as the Carrot King appearing with a 'Zing! Zap!', the way in which the Carrot King is described and the main event on which the story is based, which is taking children away in a carrotmobile and forcing them to eat carrots.
9. Answers may vary – she would probably be dressed in carrot-coloured clothes and would wear a crown of carrots like the Carrot King.

10 The genie

Question types: 3 literal; 2 inferential; 2 evaluative; 2 deductive.
1. The two boys were called Kirpal and Scott.
2. It was winter.
3. They decided to look for shelter at the train station.
4. The bottle was dirty and he wanted to see it better.
5. The food was hot and tasty.
6. They must have felt astonished, possibly frightened.
7. The wind was freezing cold and blowing fiercely.
8. Answers may vary – the genie was wearing a 'glittering blue suit'.
9. They felt warm and happy.

11 A narrow escape

Question types: 2 literal; 2 inferential; 1 evaluative; 2 deductive
1. The instructor was an experienced rafter.
2. The raft was made out of rubber.
3. Answers may vary – he may have thought that there was a danger of Lucy going overboard as they rafted around the bend.
4. He probably feared that Lucy might have drowned.
5. A rafter became a member of the Tadpole Club by falling over the side of a raft.
6. Own answer.
7. The crisis is when Lucy falls overboard and goes under the water.

Drama

12 Trouble at home

Question types: 4 literal; 3 inferential; 2 evaluative; 2 deductive
1. The two characters in the play are Joshua and Luke.
2. Joshua's dad has just lost his job.
3. He looks for jobs in the paper every morning.
4. He is going for a job interview.
5. The stage directions tell us, 'He frowns'; he says that he hopes his dad finds a job soon.
6. The conversation is taking place in mid-afternoon.
7. The boys are discussing their family problems and home life.
8. The company did not make enough money and had to lose some jobs or close down.
9. Answers may vary – the problems might be lack of money; depression; loss of self-esteem and self-respect; frequent arguments at home; people losing their temper more easily.
10. Answers may vary – people look for new jobs in advertisements in newspapers or job agencies; by visiting the Job Centre; by writing letters to employers; asking around, getting information from friends and relatives.
11. Answers may vary – it is written in dialogue form; there are no speech marks; names of speakers are in small capitals followed by a colon; it is made to sound like oral language with incomplete sentences, slang and so on.

13 **The Hare and the Tortoise**

Question types: 3 literal; 3 inferential; 2 evaluative; 1 deductive
1. The two main characters are Hare and Tortoise.
2. Hare lost the race because he went to sleep.
3. The message was 'slow and steady wins the race'.
4. Hare saying, 'No one has ever beaten me. Ever!' showed he was boastful.
5. The audience liked Tortoise more; they cheered and cried, 'Hooray for Tortoise!'
6. Hare: boastful, overconfident, scornful, fast, impatient, rude; Tortoise: steady, slow, patient, determined, persistent, wise.
7. Own answer.
8. Answers may vary – Hare is very quick and so confident in his own ability that he will probably not remember Tortoise's advice.
9. Own answer.

14 **The haunted house**

Question types: 3 literal; 1 inferential; 1 evaluative; 2 deductive
1. The play took place at night, probably just after dark.
2. They dived behind the couch.
3. Tanya was braver – she was ready to go inside the house and she switched on the torch to see the 'ghost'.
4. Tanya persuades Joanne that it's an adventure; Own answer.
5. They make the play more atmospheric; the audience cannot see what is happening so they must imagine the scene by hearing the sounds.
6. The ghost is only a cat.
7. Answers may vary – the stage directions reveal that the girls were frightened ('in a shaking voice', 'terrified', 'in a panic', 'The girls scream').

Recount

15 **First day in Year 3**

Question types: 4 literal; 3 inferential; 1 evaluative; 1 deductive
1. The writer's friend was called Ben.
2. The new teacher's name was Mr Rigg.
3. The class did some writing; Mr Rigg read a story.
4. His story was about a frightening encounter with a big snake.
5. He was the first male teacher that the writer had had.
6. Year 2 had more things around the walls.
7. The things that made the writer happy were: sitting next to Ben; Mr Rigg being really friendly; Mr Rigg reading a great story.
8. Answers may vary – you feel lonely; you don't know anyone; you have no friends; you do not know where things are.
9. Answers may vary – he wants to appear braver than he really is.

16 **A letter to Grandma**

Question types: 4 literal; 2 inferential; 1 evaluative; 4 deductive
1. The letter was sent from Jersey.
2. The flight left Manchester at 10 o'clock in the morning.
3. The flight attendant told the passengers about the plane.
4. Stephanie drank lemonade during the flight.
5. The rough air in the clouds (turbulence) made the plane bump about.
6. Stephanie thought her parents were frightened because they closed their eyes.
7. She may have been frightened too – she also closed her eyes.
8. Answers may vary – Stephanie had probably not flown before.
9. Own answer.
10. 'revved' – made the engine run quickly; 'descending' – going down.
11. Own answer.

17 A letter to a school friend

Question types: 4 literal; 3 inferential; 1 evaluative; 3 deductive
1. Danielle was staying at the Alphorn Chalet, Rue St Antoine, Beauville, Switzerland.
2. Mum, Dad and Oliver are on holiday with Danielle.
3. It was too windy to ski.
4. She normally ate lunch at the chalet.
5. They took skiing lessons to help them to ski better.
6. Even good skiers can improve.
7. Yes, the tone of her letter was that she was enjoying her holiday, and looking forward to skiing the next day if the weather improved.
8. A chalet is a hut or small house, traditionally made of wood, with a wide, overhanging roof.
9. A blizzard is a violent snowstorm.
10. Answers may vary – Switzerland, Austria, France, Italy, America and Canada are some of the countries.
11. Own answer.

Instructions

18 Scrambled eggs on toast

Question types: 3 literal; 2 inferential; 2 evaluative; 3 deductive
1. You need four eggs.
2. You would use a whisk or fork to beat the eggs.
3. You would use a medium-sized saucepan.
4. Toasting is mentioned in the recipe.
5. Butter or margarine is used so that the eggs will not stick to the pan.
6. You would sprinkle parsley on the scrambled eggs to make the dish look attractive and to add flavour.
7. To feed four people you would need eight eggs.
8. Scrambled eggs are easy to chew and to digest.
9. Answers may vary – baking, frying, boiling, stewing, roasting and so on.
10. Squeeze toothpaste onto toothbrush. Brush teeth up and down. Don't forget gums. Rinse out mouth and rinse toothbrush.

19 Tug of war

Question types: 5 literal; 2 inferential; 1 evaluative; 2 deductive
1. These instructions tell you how to play a game of tug of war.
2. You need a long thick rope with a piece of cloth tied at the halfway mark, and a line on the ground.
3. Two teams of equal numbers and size are needed to play the game.
4. A team knows when to start when they hear 'Pull!'
5. To win, a team has to pull the other team over the line.
6. The teams should be of equal number and size to make the tug of war a fair contest.
7. A thin rope might break and would be hard to hold.
8. Answers may vary – strong or heavy people would be preferable.
9. Line up runners, each with book on head; Begin race; Tell runners who drop book to go back to start; Give prize to runner who is first over line with book on head.
10. Answers may vary – possibly football, netball, cricket, rugby, basketball, hockey, volleyball.

20 **How to plant a tree**

Question types: 3 literal; 2 inferential; 3 evaluative; 2 deductive
1. You need a tree, a spade and a watering can (fertiliser, a small stake and a tree tie are also correct answers).
2. Answers may vary – you dig a hole, place the tree in the hole and water the tree lightly.
3. You need water to moisten the hole so the tree has water straight away.
4. The spade is used to dig the hole for the tree.
5. Answers may vary – the hole would need to be larger than the pot to ensure that the roots of the tree, and the attached soil, fit in the hole, and to allow you to fill the hole with earth, which will hold the tree firmly in place.
6. Packing the earth tightly around the roots would stop the tree from falling over.
7. A stake is a thin piece of wood used for holding the tree upright as it grows.
8. Compost is rich soil in which plants are grown; fertiliser is a food for plants.
9. This gives information on how many steps there are and helps the reader to keep track of how far they have read.
10. The labels help the reader to understand the instructions and they ensure that the diagrams are clear.

Report

21 **Football**

Question types: 4 literal; 2 inferential; 2 evaluative; 2 deductive
1. Another name for football is soccer.
2. A net is used behind the goalposts.
3. Yes, football is played by both girls and boys.
4. The most famous football event in the world is the World Cup.
5. The goalkeeper makes it difficult to score a goal.
6. It is the goalkeeper's job to stop the ball going into the net, so using his hands is allowed.
7. Answers may vary – football is one of the most popular games in the world and is often on TV; it is a game of skill, which girls and boys admire, but is easy to play at some level and its basic rules are simple.
8. It is played in many countries around the world and is popular all over the globe.
9. 'Olympic sport' means a sport played at the Olympic Games.
10. 'inflated with air' – filled with air; 'net' – webbed material strung between the goalposts to catch the ball when it goes into it; 'goalkeeper' – a player protecting the goal; 'forward' – a player whose job is to score goals; defend – to stop the other team from scoring.

22 **The fairy penguin**

Question types: 4 literal; 3 inferential; 1 evaluative; 3 deductive
1. The smallest penguins in the world are fairy penguins.
2. They live in the south of Australia and New Zealand.
3. The back of a fairy penguin is dark blue.
4. Fairy penguins eat small fish and squid.
5. Webbed feet would be important to help them swim.
6. They chase and catch fish and squid in the sea.
7. If penguins get covered in oil, it stops them swimming and they drown; it can also get into their stomachs and lungs, and kill the creatures that are their food.
8. Own answer.
9. Answers may vary – to protect fairy penguins we should create sanctuaries, restrict fishing or change the type of nets and lines and prevent oil spillages.
10. 'Breeding grounds' are places where fairy penguins mate and have their young.
11. live, lay, hunt.

23 **Learning to swim**

Question types: 4 literal; 4 inferential; 1 evaluative; 2 deductive
1. Many children learn to swim when they are quite young.
2. The special swimming classes are held in the school holidays at local swimming pools.
3. Children learn to swim at the shallow end.
4. To become a good, strong swimmer you need lots of lessons (and practice).
5. Answers may vary – to teach them not to be afraid; for a number of strokes correct breathing involves putting your head under the water.
6. Shallow water is more suitable so that new swimmers can touch the bottom and learn to swim without being frightened.
7. 'Doggy paddle' is a swimming stroke in which you swim like a dog, with your arms and legs bent.
8. Older children or adults who are strong swimmers swim at the deep end.
9. Answers may vary – it is good fun, it is good exercise and it could save your life one day.
10. Answers may vary – basic swimming is the ability to keep yourself afloat, while swimming really well means knowing a number of strokes and being a strong swimmer.
11. Answers may vary – the training would entail learning to be a good swimmer yourself; knowing lots of different strokes; being aware of safety rules and techniques.

Explanation

24 **Why the sea is salty**

Question types: 5 literal; 2 inferential; 1 evaluative; 2 deductive
1. Yes, salt dissolves in water.
2. Rivers carry the salt to the sea.
3. Millions of tonnes of salt are washed into the sea each year.
4. The Red Sea and the Dead Sea are easy to swim in.
5. Yes, the Red Sea is more salty than the Atlantic Ocean.
6. Yes, because more salt will be washed into the ocean.
7. Answers may vary – mud, earth, plants, fish, bones, rubbish and so on.
8. Answers may vary – sugar, honey, jelly cubes, instant coffee powder, gravy granules and so on.
9. Own answer.
10. true; false; true.

25 **How to find information in a book**

Question types: 5 literal; 2 inferential; 1 evaluative; 1 deductive
1. The title of the book is printed on the cover and the title page.
2. The contents page lists the different sections or chapters in the book and the pages where they begin.
3. Any one selected from the following sections is correct: 'Invention of the steam train'; 'The first steam trains'; 'Travel by steam train'; 'The end of the steam train era'.
4. 'The end of the steam train era' would begin on page 41.
5. A section in a book is called a chapter.
6. Finding information in a book quickly would enable you to use the information when it was needed.
7. Yes, a contents page would be helpful because it would tell you where information can be found.
8. You would find the title of the book and the author's name on a title page.
9. false; true; false; false; true.

26 Why there is lightning then thunder

Question types: 4 literal; 2 inferential; 2 evaluative; 1 deductive
1. Lightning is a giant electric spark.
2. Thunder is caused by air heating up and suddenly expanding.
3. Light travels faster than sound.
4. A flash of lightning is a long way off if the thunder is heard much later than the lightning is seen.
5. The lightning would be very close.
6. The lightning is a long way away.
7. Run to a safe place indoors (a car is very safe). If you are in a wide, open space and there is nowhere to run to, lie flat on the ground. Try to make your surroundings higher than you are (for example, by sitting down on a river bank).
8. Answers may vary – rainstorms, sandstorms, hailstorms, snowstorms, tornadoes, hurricanes.
9. false; true; true.

Argument

27 We should look after our trees

Question types: 2 literal; 2 inferential; 2 evaluative; 1 deductive
1. Answers may vary – points to cover include: trees maintain the right quality of air; they support the soil; they can be used as homes for animals and birds and give them food; they provide shade and shelter; they make the environment pleasant to look at.
2. They provide homes and food for birds and animals.
3. Trees are important in summer because they provide shade from the hot sun.
4. Answers may vary – birds and animals may eat the flowers, leaves, berries, fruit and sometimes the bark of the trees.
5. Answers may vary – all around the world forests are being cut down, so we need to protect those trees that are left and plant more of them.
6. Trees keep the air pure because they give off oxygen and take in carbon dioxide. The roots of trees hold the soil together. Trees provide homes for birds and animals. Trees keep us cool because they shade us from the hot sun. Trees are beautiful to look at.
7. Answers may vary – the balance of nature would be harmed; there would be no shade; no beautiful trees to look at; no habitat for birds and animals; soil erosion would take place.

28 Going to school

Question types: 5 literal; 3 inferential; 2 evaluative; 1 deductive
1. Children in the UK must start school at the age of five.
2. Children must attend school for eleven years.
3. When we first go to school we learn to read, to write and to work with numbers.
4. literacy; numeracy.
5. No, these skills are useful in our daily lives.
6. They will be helpful to us throughout our lives.
7. It teaches us that it is important to stay fit, strong and healthy.
8. Own answer.
9. Working together and helping each other.
10. Own answer.
11. Answers may vary – there are many jobs for which numeracy skills are required, such as jobs in shops, banks and accountancy.

29 Things were better then

Question types: 4 literal; 1 inferential; 3 evaluative; 2 deductive
1. There were fewer people living in cities in our grandparents' day.
2. The air was cleaner.
3. There were not as many cars, lorries, planes and factories as there are today.
4. Boys and girls tend to spend less time outdoors nowadays.
5. Answers may vary – there is too much traffic; too much crime; roads are too busy; land is much more built up; there are not enough cycle tracks.
6. 'All of these things make me think that life was better for boys and girls in my grandparents' day.'
7. They give off gases containing tiny particles, and these gases make the air dirty.
8. Rubbish and industrial waste are dumped in our rivers and oceans; algae forms.
9. pollution – something that makes the air, water or land dirty; industrial waste – matter that is left over from factories; algae – a type of weed that pollutes the water.
10. Own answer.

30 Travel teaches you many things

Question types: 1 literal; 1 inferential; 2 evaluative; 4 deductive
1. The first, second and fifth statements are correct.
2. Correct answers are three from the following: homes, food, clothes, jobs, transport, leisure time, language, lifestyle.
3. It is important to ask questions so that you learn more and understand better.
4. 'Lifestyle' means the way in which people live.
5. Own answer.
6. Answers may vary – the writer sums up the argument in the final paragraph, so any statements taken from that section are correct.
7 and 8. Own answers.

Read this poem

CRAYONING

The sheet of paper is white
And perfectly quiet
Like a drift of snow
Into which nobody goes
And out of which nothing shows.

Then I crayon a sun to shine
And the sky's blue line,
A red house with a green door
And a chimney above it all
Out of which the black smoke pours.

In the garden is a mother
Hanging out clothes of every colour;
And flowers of every colour grow
Where once the paper
Was white as snow.

Stanley Cook

Re-read the poem

Answer the following questions.
(Use the back of the sheet for questions 4 to 8.)

1. How does the poem describe a sheet of paper? _____

_____

2. Think of two more words that would describe a sheet of paper. _____

_____

3. Whose clothes might you see hanging on the line? _____

_____

4. Write down the pair of words in each verse that rhyme.
5. Which pair of words sounds the same but doesn't look the same?
6. Why is the sheet of paper **like a drift of snow into which nobody goes**?
7. What do you like about a clean sheet of paper?
8. What other things could the poem have in the garden?

Read this poem ➤

JOHN AND JIM

I've got a secret friend
Who lives at home with me.
Even when we're talking
There's no one there to see.
My name's John and his name's Jim.
You can see me, but you can't see him.

I've got a secret friend
Who goes to school with me.
Even when we're walking
There's no one there to see.
My name's John and his name's Jim.
You can see me, but you can't see him.

I've got a secret friend
Who sits in class with me.
Even when we're writing
There's no one there to see.
My name's John and his name's Jim.
You can see me, but you can't see him.

I've got a secret friend
Who likes to box with me.
Even when we're fighting
There's no one there to see.
My name's John and his name's Jim.
You can see me, but you can't see him.

Barbara Ireson and Christopher Rowe

Re-read the poem ➤ **Use the back of the sheet to answer the following questions.**

1. What is John's secret friend called?
2. Why is this friend kept secret by John?
3. How do you think they can box together?
4. Why can't the secret friend be seen?
5. Where does John's secret friend live?
6. What are the things the friends do together?
7. Which words in the poem rhyme with **talking** and **writing**?
8. Why do you think John has a secret friend?

Read this poem →

THE WITCHES' RIDE

Over the hills
Where the edge of the light
Deepens and darkens
To ebony night,
Narrow hats high
Above yellow bead eyes,
The tatter-haired witches
Ride through the skies.
Over the seas
Where the flat fishes sleep
Wrapped in the slap of the slippery deep,
Over the peaks
Where the black trees are bare,
Where bony birds quiver
They glide through the air.
Silently humming
A horrible tune,
They sweep through the stillness
To sit on the moon.

Karla Kuskin

Re-read the poem →

Answer the following questions.
(Use the back of the sheet for questions 5 to 10.)

1. Who is the poem about? _____

2. What are the witches doing? _____

3. What time of day is it in the poem? _____

4. Describe how you think the witches look. _____

_____

5. Where are the witches going?
6. What do you think the witches are riding on?
7. Why is the word **ebony** used to describe the night?
8. Write down the pairs of words that rhyme.
9. What do you think is the **slippery deep**?
10. What might be horrible about the tune the witches hummed?

Read this poem ➤

WATER

Water has no taste at all,
  Water has no smell;
Water's in the waterfall,
  In pump, and tap, and well.

Water's every where about;
  Water's in the rain,
In the bath, the pond, and out
  At sea it's there again.

Water comes into my eyes
  And down my cheeks in tears,
When Mother cries, "Go back and try
  To wash behind those ears."

John R Crossland

Re-read the poem ➤

Answer the following questions.
(Use the back of the sheet for questions 4 to 10.)

1. List the places in which the poem says water is found. _____

_____

_____

2. Write down two other places in which water can be found. _____

_____

3. Why do you think the writer cries when he is told to wash behind his ears? _____

_____

4. How does the poem describe what water is like?
5. Write down two more ways of describing water.
6. **Smell** and **well** rhyme. Write down four more pairs of words that rhyme.
7. What do you use water for in your home?
8. Why has the poet's mother said, **"Wash behind those ears"**?
9. Where else is water used in town and in the country?
10. Make a list of animals that live in water.

Read this poem →

BONES

Bones is good with children,
He goes with us everywhere;
The beach, the park, the swimming-pool,
He comes to look us up at school –
He's stopped the Dodgems at the Fair.

Bones is good with children,
He does the same things as us;
Won't wipe his feet, won't shut the gate,
Goes off all day, then trails home late,
To "Bad", and bed, and fuss…

Bones is good with children,
He gets muddy and then he pongs
Of earth and burn and wood and pond,
The hills and all the moors beyond –
When it rains he rolls his eyes and longs

To be out with the children
And gets himself soaked through,
Slide down the banks on tea-trays,
Chase sticks, and join our football-frays –
I think he'll even come with you:

'Cos Bones is good with children!

Brian Lee

Continued on **P97** →

Re-read the poem **Answer the following questions.**

1. What or who is Bones? _____

   _____

2. Who is Bones good with? _____

   _____

3. What did Bones stop at the Fair? _____

   _____

4. Where do you think Bones lives, in the town or in the country? _____

   _____

5. Does Bones make a good companion for children? _____

   _____

6. What does Bones do when the children are at school? _____

   _____

7. What happens when Bones comes in late without wiping his feet? _____

   _____

   _____

8. Who do you think says **"Bad"** to Bones? _____

   _____

9. Is Bones trustworthy and friendly? _____

   _____

10. How do you think Bones got his name? _____

    _____

Continued from P96

Read this story ➤

THE FIRST CHICK

"What are you doing?" Claudius complained one morning. "If you bounce on my feet any more you'll plant me in the snow and I'll never move again. And stop waving your flippers about like that. It feels like a blizzard blowing up there."

Otto didn't stop. "I'm trying to fly," he shouted. "You said I'm a bird. Birds fly, don't they?"

"Penguins don't fly," Claudius said. "Now stop jumping on my feet and I'll tell you what penguins do."

Otto stopped. He was getting tired anyway. "What do penguins do?" he asked, a little breathlessly.

"They swim. That's like flying in the sea. They're very good at it too."

Otto looked up at Claudius.

"I want to fly up high like that bird up there. It's going round and round in the sky, and I want to do that."

"Well you can't, so don't start bouncing again. Anyway, what bird?" Claudius was looking up. "Oh my goodness, a skua. Now stay close to me, Otto. Nasty things, skuas. They like chicks."

Otto was puzzled. "Are you nasty then, Claudius?"

"Am I…? Oh I see! I like chicks but not for dinner. A skua will dive down from the sky and steal a nice juicy penguin chick for its next meal."

Jill Tomlinson

 **Re-read the story** ➤

Answer the following questions.
(Use the back of the sheet for questions 4 to 8.)

1. What was Otto doing? _____

_____

2. What did Otto want to do? _____

3. What do penguins use to swim with? _____

4. Why was the skua flying in circles overhead?
5. Where do you think Claudius and Otto are?
6. What was puzzling Otto?
7. How does Claudius feel about seeing a skua flying overhead?
8. Do you think Otto is good at working things out for himself?

Read this story ➤

THE OWL WHO WAS AFRAID OF THE DARK

Plop was a baby Barn Owl, and he lived with his Mummy and Daddy at the top of a very tall tree in a field.

Plop was fat and fluffy.

He had a beautiful heart-shaped ruff.

He had enormous, round eyes.

He had very knackety knees.

In fact he was exactly the same as every baby Barn Owl that has ever been – except for one thing.

Plop was afraid of the dark.

"You *can't* be afraid of the dark," said his Mummy. "Owls are never afraid of the dark."

"This one is," Plop said.

"But owls are *night* birds," she said.

Plop looked down at his toes. "I don't want to be a night bird," he mumbled. "I want to be a day bird."

"You are what you are," said Mrs Barn Owl firmly.

"Yes, I know," agreed Plop, "and what I are is afraid of the dark."

"Oh dear," said Mrs Barn Owl. It was clear that she was going to need a lot of patience. She shut her eyes and tried to think how best she could help Plop not to be afraid. Plop waited.

His mother opened her eyes again. "Plop, you are only afraid of the dark because you don't know about it."

Jill Tomlinson

Re-read the story ➤

Answer the following questions.
(Use the back of the sheet for questions 3 to 8.)

1. What sort of bird was Plop? _____

2. What made Plop different from other birds like him? _____

_____

3. Why are owls called night birds?
4. Why will Mrs Barn Owl need a lot of patience?
5. Why does Plop want to be a day bird?
6. Do you think Plop's mother was right about why Plop was afraid of the dark?
7. Why wouldn't Plop know about the dark?
8. How will Plop get over his fear of the dark?

Read this story

URSULA BEAR

Ursula was so fond of bears that she thought about very little else, and she had a very special secret that hardly anybody knew about. She knew how to turn herself into a real live bear by means of a simple magic spell. She had found the spell in a book in the library and it really worked. Ursula had turned herself into a small brown bear for a whole day and a night and being a bear was wonderful, but it had got her into so much trouble that she thought she had better never do it again.

One Friday afternoon when Ursula was on her way home from her dancing lesson at Miss Jardine's, a large coloured poster in the window of the sweet shop caught her eye. It was a picture of two enormous polar bears, and as Ursula read the poster her eyes grew round.

"Bears!" breathed Ursula. "Performing polar bears!" She ran all the way home without stopping once. The kitchen was full of the warm treacly smell of baking gingerbread and Aunt Prudence was there wearing a yellow apron and a smudge of flour on her nose. She blinked in surprise when she saw Ursula.

"Goodness, child! You look quite out of breath," she said.

Sheila Lavelle

Re-read the story

Answer the following questions.
(Use the back of the sheet for questions 4 to 8.)

1. What was Ursula so fond of? _____

2. Where had Ursula been on Friday afternoon? _____

_____

3. Why would Ursula want to turn herself into a bear? _____

_____

4. What event could the poster be advertising?
5. What sort of person do you think Aunt Prudence was?
6. How did Aunt Prudence get flour on her nose?
7. Why might Ursula not use the spell again?
8. How difficult was it to turn into a bear?

Read this story

THE TWITS

Once a week, on Wednesdays, the Twits had Bird Pie for supper. Mr Twit caught the birds and Mrs Twit cooked them.

Mr Twit was good at catching birds. On the day before Bird Pie day, he would put the ladder up against The Big Dead Tree and climb into the branches with a bucket of glue and a paint-brush. The glue he used was something called HUGTIGHT and it was stickier than any other glue in the world. He would paint it along the tops of all the branches and then go away.

As the sun went down, birds would fly in from all around to roost for the night in The Big Dead Tree. They didn't know, poor things, that the branches were all smeared with horrible HUGTIGHT. The moment they landed on a branch, their feet stuck and that was that.

The next morning, which was Bird Pie day, Mr Twit would climb up the ladder again and grab all the wretched birds that were stuck to the tree. It didn't matter what kind they were – song thrushes, blackbirds, sparrows, crows, little jenny wrens, robins, anything – they all went into the pot for Wednesday's Bird Pie supper.

Roald Dahl

 **Re-read the story**

Answer the following questions.
(Use the back of the sheet for questions 3 to 8.)

1. What did the Twits have for supper on Wednesdays? _____

_____

2. Which tree did Mr Twit climb into? _____

_____

3. On what day would Mr Twit put glue on the branches of the tree?
4. Why would the birds roost in The Big Dead Tree?
5. Do you think the birds would learn not to roost in the tree?
6. What do you think gave Mr Twit the idea to put glue on the branches?
7. What would Mrs Twit have to do to the birds before she cooked them?
8. How do you think Mr Twit feels about wildlife?

Read this story

A BIRTHDAY FOR FRANCES

It was the day before Frances's little sister Gloria's birthday. Mother and Gloria were sitting at the kitchen table, making place cards for the party. Frances was in the broom closet, singing:

"Happy Thursday to you,
Happy Thursday to you,
Happy Thursday, dear Alice,
Happy Thursday to you."

"Who is Alice?" asked Mother.

"Alice is somebody that nobody can see," said Frances. "And that is why she does not have a birthday. So I am singing Happy Thursday to her."

"Today is Friday," said Mother.

"It is Thursday for Alice," said Frances. "Alice will not have h-r-n-d, and she will not have g-k-l-s. But we are singing together."

"What are h-r-n-d and g-k-l-s?" asked Mother.

"Cake and candy. I thought you could spell," said Frances.

"I am sure that Alice will have cake and candy on her birthday," said Mother.

"But Alice does not have a birthday," said Frances.

"Yes, she does," said Mother. "Even if nobody can see her, Alice has one birthday every year, and so do you. Your birthday is two months from now. Then you will be the birthday girl. But tomorrow is Gloria's birthday, and she will be the birthday girl."

"That is how it is, Alice," said Frances. "Your birthday is always the one that is not now."

Russell Hoban

Continued on P103

Re-read the story ➤ **Answer the following questions.**

1. Who was sitting at the kitchen table? _____

_____

2. Where was Frances? _____

_____

3. Who is the older girl, Frances or Gloria? _____

_____

4. Why doesn't Alice have a birthday? _____

_____

5. Why can't anyone see Alice? _____

_____

6. Why does Frances use the letters **h-r-n-d** and **g-k-l-s** to spell **cake** and **candy**?

_____

_____

7. Do you think this story is written for people in this country? _____

_____

_____

8. Do you think Frances often plays on her own? _____

_____

_____

Continued from P102 ➤

Read this story

No Roses for Harry

Harry was a white dog with black spots. On his birthday, he got a present from Grandma. It was a woollen sweater with roses on it. Harry didn't like it the moment he saw it. He didn't like the roses.

When he tried it on, he felt cosy and snug. But he still didn't like the roses. He thought it was the silliest sweater he'd ever seen.

The next day when Harry went into town with the children, he wore his new sweater. When people saw it, they laughed. When dogs saw it, they barked. Harry made up his mind then and there to lose Grandma's present.

When they went into a big store to shop, the children took off his sweater and let him carry it. This was just what Harry wanted. First he tried to lose it in the pet department – but a man found it and gave it back. Then he tried to lose it in the grocery department – but a lady found it and gave it back. He tried to lose it in the flower department – but a little boy found it and gave it back. The children didn't let Harry carry it any more. They made him wear it. As they started home, Harry was beginning to think he'd never lose it.

When he got home, his friends were waiting to play with him. But Harry didn't feel like playing so they left him alone. As he sat wondering what to do, Harry noticed a loose stitch in his sweater. He pulled at the wool – just a little at first – then a bit more – and a little bit more. Harry didn't know it, but a bird was watching.

In a minute, Harry had pulled out quite a long piece of the wool. The end of it lay on the grass behind him. Suddenly the bird flew down. Quick as a flash she took the end of the wool in her beak and flew away with it! It all happened before Harry could even blink. The sweater began to disappear right before Harry's eyes.

Gene Zion

Continued on P105

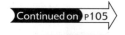

Re-read the story

Answer the following questions.

1. What did Harry look like? _____

_____

2. Who gave Harry a woollen sweater? _____

_____

3. Why didn't Harry like the roses? _____

_____

4. What was good about the sweater? _____

_____

5. Why was it so difficult to lose the sweater in the shop? _____

_____

_____

6. Why did the children make Harry wear the sweater when they came out of
the shop?

_____

7. Why didn't Harry feel like playing with his friends? _____

_____

8. What would happen when the bird flew away with the end of the wool? _____

_____

9. Do you think Harry meant the bird to take the end of the wool? _____

_____

10. What sort of sweater would suit Harry better? _____

_____

Continued from P104

Read this story ►

CHARLIE AND THE CHOCOLATE FACTORY

Charlie Bucket stared around the gigantic room in which he now found himself. The place was like a witch's kitchen! All about him black metal pots were boiling and bubbling on huge stoves, and kettles were hissing and pans were sizzling, and strange iron machines were clanking and spluttering, and there were pipes running all over the ceiling and walls, and the whole place was filled with smoke and steam and delicious rich smells.

Mr Wonka himself had suddenly become even more excited than usual, and anyone could see that this was the room he loved best of all. He was hopping about among the saucepans and the machines like a child among his Christmas presents, not knowing which thing to look at first. He lifted the lid from a huge pot and took a sniff; then he rushed over and dipped a finger into a barrel of sticky yellow stuff and had a taste; then he skipped across to one of the machines and turned half a dozen knobs this way and that; then he peered anxiously through the glass door of a gigantic oven, rubbing his hands and cackling with delight at what he saw inside. Then he ran over to another machine, a small shiny affair that kept going *phut-phut-phut-phut-phut*, and every time it went *phut*, a large green marble dropped out of it into a basket on the floor. At least it looked like a marble.

"Everlasting Gobstoppers!" cried Mr Wonka proudly. "They're completely new! I am inventing them for children who are given very little pocket money. You can put an Everlasting Gobstopper in your mouth and you can suck it and suck it and suck it and suck it and it will *never* get any smaller!"

"It's like gum!" cried Violet Beauregarde.

"It is *not* like gum," Mr Wonka said, "Gum is for chewing, and if you tried chewing one of these Gobstoppers here you'd break your teeth off! And they never get any smaller! They never disappear! NEVER! At least I don't think they do. There's one of them being tested this very moment in the Testing Room next door…"

Roald Dahl

Continued on ►P107 ►

Re-read the story **Answer the following questions.**

1. What was the room that Charlie Bucket found himself in like? _____

_____

2. Why had Mr Wonka become so excited? _____

_____

3. What was making the delicious rich smells? _____

_____

4. Why was Mr Wonka hopping about among the saucepans and machines?

_____

5. Why did Violet think that an Everlasting Gobstopper was like chewing gum?

_____

_____

6. Why would children with very little pocket money like Everlasting Gobstoppers?

_____

_____

7. How long would you expect an Everlasting Gobstopper to last? _____

_____

8. Could Mr Wonka be called an inventor? _____

_____

9. Was Charlie surprised at the gigantic room? _____

_____

10. Why did the Everlasting Gobstopper look like a marble? _____

_____

Continued from P106

Read this play →

TREASURE TROVE

SCENE 1

Ed and Will are playing football near a hedge in the park. Will has kicked the ball over the hedge.

ED: Hey! That was a good shot!

WILL: It's OK – we'll squeeze through the hedge.

(The boys crawl through the hedge and look for the ball.)

ED: Look, it's stuck on a spike in this rabbit hole. Oh, it's got a puncture now.

WILL: Look! There's a bag stuffed in the hole! What's in it?

ED: Wow! It's some silver plates and a dagger!

WILL: It's a treasure trove – we'll be rich!

ED: We'd better take it to the police. We can't say 'finders keepers' with this lot!

SCENE 2

Down at the police station, the sergeant is looking at their find.

WILL: Is it a treasure trove? It was just dumped in the hole.

SERG: Well it could be – it was put there on purpose to be collected later. It would have to be solid silver though. It looks like the things stolen from the Browns. If it is, they will be glad to have it back. I expect they'll give you a reward.

ED: Great! We'll be able to buy a new football!

Re-read the play →   **Answer the following questions on the back of the sheet.**

1. What were the two boys doing in the park?
2. What had Will done?
3. What punctured the football?
4. Why do you think the boys took their find to the police station?
5. What two things would make their find a treasure trove?
6. Do you think the Browns will give the boys a reward?
7. Do you think the boys were right to take their find to the police station?
8. What does **solid silver** mean?

Read this recount

MY NEW SCHOOL

My dad is a policeman. We did live in London but Dad got a transfer to a new job at a police station in Dorset. We moved in the summer holidays. It was sad leaving my friends at school but we have promised to write to each other.

I started my new school this week. The boys and other girls in my class are nice. One girl called Selina said I could play with her. She has got a lot of friends and she lives near my new house.

Selina has always lived in Dorset. It was funny when she asked me where I lived. She said, "Where are you to?" and I didn't understand what she meant! It made us laugh! I told her about things people say in London like "apples and pears" for stairs. Selina thought that was funny too!

Our teacher told us about the after-school clubs. I played the recorder at my last school so he said I could join the recorder group.

Mum says I can ask Selina round to play on Saturday and have tea. I am going to write to my friend Katharine to tell her all about it.

Re-read the play

Answer the following questions.
(Use the back of the sheet for questions 5 to 8.)

1. What job does the writer's dad do? _____

2. Where is his new job? _____

3. Do you think the writer is a girl or a boy? _____

_____

4. What do you think the phrase **"Where are you to?"** means? _____

_____

5. Do you think Selina will make a good friend?
6. Do you think the writer will be happy at the new school?
7. How will having Selina round for tea help the writer?
8. Why is it a good thing that the writer can play the recorder?

Read this recipe ➤

FRUIT AND CHEESE KEBABS

These kebabs are fun to make for your friends when they come for tea.

You will need about 150g of firm cheese. You can use Cheddar cheese, Double Gloucester and Red Leicester cheese. The different cheeses will add colour to your kebabs.

You will also need a small bunch of green grapes and one of black grapes, a small tin of pineapple chunks, a small tin of mandarin oranges and a bundle of wooden kebab skewers or cocktail sticks.

Remember to wash your hands before you touch the food!

Drain the juice from the tins of fruit. (You can put this in a glass to drink.)

Cut the cheese into 2cm cubes. Wash the grapes and pat them dry with kitchen paper.

Thread the fruit and cheese cubes carefully on to the skewers. Decide what order looks the best and make all the skewers the same.

You can stick the end of each kebab into a hard cabbage cut in half. This looks good on a plate in the middle of the table for your friends to help themselves.

You can experiment with different fruits and vegetables that go well with cheese.

Continued on P111 ➤

Re-read the recipe

Answer the following questions.

1. Write out a shopping list of the things you need to make the kebabs. _____

_____

_____

_____

2. What sequence of fruit and cheese do you think would look attractive? _____

_____

_____

3. Why do you need to use firm cheese? _____

_____

4. What must you always do before touching food? _____

_____

5. Which would make better kebabs – kebab skewers or cocktail sticks? _____

_____

_____

6. Write down three other things that you think could go on the kebabs. _____

_____

7. Why is it important to wash the grapes? _____

_____

8. What would happen if you didn't drain the tinned fruit well or dry the grapes?

_____

_____

Continued from P110

Read these instructions

FIRST AID FOR A GRAZED KNEE

A graze can happen when a person slides along the ground as they fall and the top layer of skin is scraped away. If the fall happens outside, there may be dirt in the wound.

To give first aid to the person who is hurt, you will need a bowl of warm water, some cotton wool balls, a packet of sterile gauze and adhesive tape or adhesive dressings.

First, wash your hands before you start to give first aid. Then wet a ball of cotton wool in the water and gently bathe the grazed area to wash away any dirt or grit that is in the wound. Use a fresh piece of cotton wool each time you wipe the graze.

When all the dirt has been cleaned away, blot the wound with a piece of sterile gauze to mop up any water and blood.

If the graze is large, cover it with a sterile gauze dressing and fasten it in place with strips of adhesive tape. If the graze is small, use an adhesive dressing that is large enough to cover the wound.

It is important to keep the wound clean so that it does not become infected.

Re-read the instructions

Answer the following questions.
(Use the back of the sheet for questions 4 to 8.)

1. How could you graze yourself? _____

_____

2. Why do you need to be gentle when bathing a graze? _____

_____

3. What do you need to give first aid to someone with a graze? _____

_____

_____

4. Why is it useful to know about first aid?
5. Which of these phrases means **sterile**: brand new, germ free, scratchy?
6. What might happen if the graze isn't properly cleaned?
7. What other accidents can happen around the home?
8. What should you do if a really bad accident happened?

Scholastic Literacy Skills
Comprehension Ages 8–9

SCHOLASTIC Photocopiable

Read this report

DUNSTON PRIMARY SCHOOL PTA

The Parent–Teacher Association for Dunston Primary School organises events to raise money for the school. Every year, the chairperson of the PTA *writes a report about what they have been doing. This is the report for last year.*

We have had a busy year and I am pleased to report that our events have raised the sum of £2117.

The year began with a jumble sale which raised £336. The Hallowe'en barn dance went well and 153 tickets were sold at £3 each. The refreshments and bar made another £187. The Christmas fête was in December and the school Christmas cards sold well. The total made was £420. The spring term began with a bingo evening. This raised £347 with the raffle. Sponsored swims and bicycle rides raised £302 and the sale of printed tea towels has brought in £66 so far.

The staff have asked if the PTA will buy a colour printer, a crash mat and a video recorder. Money for the Christmas play costumes and the children's party would be welcomed. We shall pay for a lifeguard for swimming as usual. Any money left over will be spent on library books.

Thank you all for your hard work.

Re-read the report

Answer the following questions on the back of the sheet.

1. What do the letters PTA stand for?
2. How many events did the PTA organise during the year?
3. What other events could the PTA have held?
4. How much did the barn dance make altogether?
5. Which event raised the most money?
6. Why is a lifeguard needed at swimming?
7. What sort of parent would belong to the PTA?
8. Do you think the money has been well spent? What other items might be useful for the school?
9. What sponsored events have you or your school taken part in?

Read this report ➤

THE PLAYGROUND

A newspaper report tells us about things that have happened around the world. The reporters for local newspapers tell readers about things that have happened in their own area. Here is a report about a local playground.

Dunston County Council has improved the old playground by replacing the worn-out equipment and adding new pieces. This was made possible by a grant from the National Lottery.

Children using the playground were asked what they would like. The old swings have been painted and six new swings have been added for toddlers. A new slide and playhouse have been built next to the sandpit and the roundabout has been painted. A new see-saw and rocking horse complete the play equipment. Rubber tiles have been put round each piece of equipment and the whole playground has been fenced in. A notice to say only children under 14 years can use the playground has been put on the gate.

The official opening of the playground was well attended by parents and children, including Helen and Matthew Jones who said they were very pleased with the new playground.

Re-read the report ➤

Answer the following questions.
(Use the back of the sheet for questions 3 to 8.)

1. What does a reporter for a local newspaper write about? _____

_____

_____

2. What is next to the sandpit? _____

_____

3. Why should the playground be for children under 14 years only?
4. What are the rubber tiles for?
5. How safe do you think the playground will be?
6. How useful is this report to local people?
7. Who looks after the playground?
8. Where did the money for the playground come from?

Read this explanation →

TOOTHPASTE

In the 1870s, people who cleaned their teeth used a tooth powder. The tooth powder was made of burnt eggshells, cuttlefish bone or coral that had been ground up to a fine powder.

The toothpaste we have today is made of ten or more different things. Some toothpaste is made of powdered chalk. The chalk is a little bit gritty. The grit helps to remove the layer left on our teeth by the food and drink we have had. This layer also has plaque in it. The bacteria in the plaque decay our teeth.

The powdered chalk is made into a paste by mixing it with water. The paste is then mixed with something to make it thick. A very tiny drop of detergent is added to make the toothpaste foamy, which helps to clean our teeth. To make the toothpaste taste nice, a little peppermint oil is mixed into it. Most toothpaste has fluoride in it. Fluoride helps to make the enamel on our teeth strong so they are not so easily decayed.

The toothpaste tubes are filled through the wide end. When the tube is full, the end is pressed flat and crimped to seal it.

Re-read the explanation →

Answer the following questions.
(Use the back of the sheet for questions 4 to 8.)

1. What was toothpaste made of in the 1870s? _____

_____

2. What might decay our teeth? _____

_____

3. How does the grit in toothpaste clean our teeth? _____

_____

4. Is toothpaste without any fluoride as good as toothpaste containing it?
5. How would foam help to clean teeth?
6. What other flavours could you use to make toothpaste taste nice?
7 What do sticky sweets do to teeth?
8. Which part of a tooth is made of enamel?

Read this explanation →

WATER

Some of our houses use a lot of water. Most people have washing machines to wash their clothes, and many people now have dishwashers to do all the washing up. These machines use gallons of water. We also use a lot of water when we have showers, baths and flush lavatories.

All the water we use in our homes and schools comes from rainwater in the first place. The rain that falls fills the rivers and lakes. Rainwater trickles down through the ground and fills wells and underground springs. With all the water we use in our homes, we need plenty of rain!

We need water to drink as well as for our machines. The water in the rivers or lakes is not clean or safe enough to drink. The water that comes to our houses has to be cleaned and made safe for us to drink and use for cooking.

To make water safe, it is pumped from the rivers or lakes and kept in a reservoir. A reservoir is a specially made lake. The water goes into the reservoir through a screen. This screen is like a net and traps all the leaves, twigs and branches that may be floating in the water.

The water then trickles down through layers of sand and gravel. Any tiny plants and bits that are still in the water are left behind. The water that trickles through is now quite clean. Chlorine is added to kill any germs that may be in the water. Now the water is safe for us to drink.

Continued on P117

SCHOLASTIC Photocopiable

Re-read the explanation   **Answer the following questions.**

1. What do we use water for in our houses? _____

_____

2. Where does the water we use come from in the first place? _____

_____

3. What else do we use water for? _____

_____

4. What would happen if it didn't rain? _____

_____

5. What else might be in river water apart from twigs, leaves and branches? _____

_____

_____

6. What might happen to us if we drank water with germs in it? _____

_____

7. Do you think we need to use water that is fit to drink for our showers, baths and lavatories?

_____

8. What would we need to do to sea water to be able to use it? _____

_____

9. Is the water in your house clear and nice to drink? _____

_____

10. What is a reservoir used for? _____

_____

Continued from P116

Read this explanation

THE LIBRARY

A library is a collection of books. If you have books at home, that is your own library. It will have the books that interest you.

Your school library has books that you all need for your school work. There are also story books for you to read and enjoy.

A public library has books for everyone to use and borrow. If your public library doesn't have a book you need, it can be borrowed from another public library for you.

Books can be divided into two big groups: there are fiction books, which are made-up stories, and there are non-fiction books, which are about things that are true.

Non-fiction books are divided into subject groups such as birds, sport, music and so on. Each subject has a different number. This is to help you find the book you need. These subject groups were worked out by an American librarian called Melvil Dewey in 1876. Books have been grouped like this in most libraries ever since. A 'Dewey number' is put on the spine of each non-fiction book and it has its own special place on the shelves.

Re-read the explanation

Answer the following questions.
(Use the back of the sheet for questions 3 to 8.)

1. Who would use a public library? _____

_____

2. What is a collection of books called? _____

_____

3. Who put non-fiction books into the subject groups?
4. Would a book about computers be fiction or non-fiction?
5. What does a Dewey number tell you?
6. How long have non-fiction books been grouped by subject?
7. Is it a good idea to separate fiction books from non-fiction books in a library?
8. How useful do you think a public library is?

SCHOLASTIC Photocopiable

Read this argument →

EARLY TO BED

Many children make a fuss when they are told to go to bed. This happens whether they are sent to bed early or late!

Resting in bed is important for growing children. Children have usually been very busy during the day. They run about when they are playing and doing sports at school. Resting in bed gives a child's body the chance to relax.

Relaxing is important for bones and muscles. By the end of a busy day, the cells of young bones get squeezed together because they are not as hard as adult bones. Resting in bed lets the bones stretch out again. The muscles of the body become tired. Resting lets the muscles get their energy back.

The brain has also been working hard all day. This makes it tired. The best way for the brain to rest is by sleeping. Young children need about 12 hours sleep each night to keep healthy. As people get older, they need less sleep.

When people get tired, their brains don't work as well and accidents can happen. There is a lot of truth in the saying "Early to bed, early to rise makes a man healthy, wealthy and wise"!

Re-read the argument →

Answer the following questions.
(Use the back of the sheet for questions 4 to 8.)

1. What do many children do when they are told to go to bed? _____

_____

2. How many hours sleep does a young child need? _____

_____

3. Why don't children like going to bed? _____

_____

4. What will make the brain tired?
5. What sort of accident could happen if someone is tired?
6. Does an adult skeleton need the same rest as a child's?
7. Do you think the saying **"Early to bed, early to rise..."** is true?
8. What time do you think you should be in bed?

Read this argument

DENTAL HYGIENE

Our teeth are one of the most important organs in our bodies. They grind up the food we eat so that we can swallow it easily. If you have ever swallowed a lump of food by mistake you will know how it can hurt! Grinding up the food also helps us to digest it.

Our "milk teeth" are our first teeth. A baby usually gets its first tooth before it is one year old. These "milk teeth" are replaced by our permanent or second teeth. You often see boys and girls of six or seven years old with their front teeth missing. These seem to be the first to come and the first to fall out!

It is important to take great care of your teeth. If they are not cleaned regularly, the food left on them becomes acid. The acid will make the teeth go bad and decay. This means that the enamel on the outside of your teeth develops holes as the decay works through. This will make your teeth ache and hurt badly.

Brushing your teeth gets rid of the little bits of food left on them. It is best to brush your teeth after every meal. Your teeth should be brushed up from the gums to the top of the teeth, not from side to side. This is to make sure the food stuck between your teeth is cleaned out.

It is difficult to brush your teeth after a midday meal if you are at school all day, but you can wash your mouth out with water – this is better than doing nothing. The most important time to clean your teeth is before you go to bed when you have finished eating for the day.

Parents can help children get into the habit of cleaning their teeth. When a baby's first milk teeth appear, a parent should gently brush the teeth with a soft brush specially made for babies. If you take good care of your teeth by keeping them clean and going to the dentist, your teeth will last a lifetime.

Continued on P121

Re-read the argument ➤ **Answer the following questions.**

1. What are a baby's first teeth called? _____

_____

2. What will happen if teeth are not kept clean? _____

_____

3. Why are our teeth important to us? _____

_____

4. How does rinsing your teeth help if you can't brush them? _____

_____

5. Do you think you need to brush your teeth after each meal? _____

_____

6. Why is it difficult to brush your teeth at school? _____

_____

7. What would happen if a tooth decayed? _____

_____

8. Do you think looking after your teeth is a good thing? _____

_____

9. Why do you think the first teeth are called **milk** teeth? _____

_____

10. Why would brushing your teeth from side to side not be good enough to clean your teeth?

_____

_____

Continued from ▶ P120

■SCHOLASTIC **Photocopiable**

Read this argument

SAVING WILD FLOWERS

Wild flowers are gradually disappearing from the countryside. Many farmers still use weedkillers or herbicides to make sure their crops are good. They think of wild flowers as weeds. Nowadays, people try to save the wild flowers that grow in meadows and hedgerows.

Part of a garden can be left as a wild garden. In this area, the common wild flowers will grow easily such as dandelions, daisies, sowthistles and buttercups. These are strong plants and they can grow almost anywhere. They are unlikely to become extinct.

Some of the rarer wild flowers will only grow in certain parts of the country. The pretty corn marigold likes sandy soil, and the lovely blue chicory likes chalky soil, so you find these plants growing well in the right place for them. But sickle hare's ear is very rare. It can only be found in one place – in the roadside grass near a village called Ongar.

Because the rarer wild flowers are so fussy about where they grow, it makes it difficult to grow them in your garden if they don't like the soil. The rarer wild plants that grow where you live may do well in your garden if you scatter some of the seeds. If everyone did this, we could be sure that our wild flowers would not disappear.

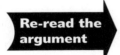

Re-read the argument   **Answer the following questions on the back of the sheet.**

1. Which wild flowers are unlikely to disappear and become extinct?
2. What do some farmers think of the wild flowers growing in their crops?
3. Why do you think wild flowers should be protected?
4. What can someone with a garden do to help stop wild flowers from disappearing?
5. What makes it difficult to stop the rarer wild flowers from disappearing?
6. What problems could a gardener have with a wild garden area?
7. Who, apart from farmers, might be causing the wild flowers to disappear?
8. What could you do to find out which wild flowers grow best where you live?

Poetry

1 Crayoning

Question types: 2 literal, 2 inferential, 2 evaluative, 2 deductive
1. The poem describes the paper as white, quiet and like a drift of snow.
2. Answers may vary – the words 'smooth', 'clean', 'fresh', 'blank', 'new' and 'plain' would describe paper.
3. You might see adults' clothes and children's clothes hanging on the line.
4. The words that rhyme are 'goes' and 'shows', 'shine' and 'line', 'grow' and 'snow'.
5. The words 'goes' and 'shows' sound the same but look different.
6. The sheet of paper has not been used.
7 and 8. Own answers.

2 John and Jim

Question types: 2 literal, 2 inferential, 2 evaluative, 2 deductive
1. John's secret friend is called Jim.
2. Own answer.
3. John could box his own shadow, which could be Jim.
4. Jim can't be seen because he isn't real.
5. John's secret friend lives at home with him.
6. They talk, walk and fight together.
7. 'Walking' rhymes with 'talking' and 'fighting' rhymes with 'writing'.
8. Own answer.

3 The Witches' Ride

Question types: 3 literal, 2 inferential, 2 evaluative, 3 deductive
1. The poem is about witches.
2. They are riding through the skies.
3. It is night-time.
4. Own answer.
5. The witches are going to the moon.
6. Answers may vary – they are probably riding on broomsticks.
7. The word 'ebony' is used because the night is black.
8. The pairs of words that rhyme are 'light' and 'night', 'eyes' and 'skies', 'sleep' and 'deep', 'bare' and 'air', 'tune' and 'moon'.
9. Answers may vary – the 'slippery deep' refers to the depth of the sea or the sea-bed.
10. Own answer.

4 Water

Question types: 2 literal, 1 inferential, 2 evaluative, 5 deductive
1. Water is found in the waterfall, the pump, the tap, the well, the rain, the bath, the pond, at sea and in tears.
2. Answers may vary – water can be found in lakes and rivers.
3. Own answer.
4. It says water has no taste or smell.
5. Answers may vary – water is clear and liquid.
6. Four more pairs of words that rhyme are 'all' and 'waterfall', 'about' and 'out', 'rain' and 'again', 'tears' and 'ears'.
7. Own answer.
8. He has dirt behind his ears.
9. Answers may vary – it is used in car washes, by the fire service and to irrigate crops.
10. Answers may vary – frogs, newts, fish, water insects, crocodiles and alligators live in water.

5 **Bones**

Question types: 2 literal, 3 inferential, 2 evaluative, 3 deductive
1. Bones is a dog.
2. Bones is good with children.
3. He stopped the dodgems.
4. He lives in the country.
5. Own answer.
6. He goes to school to look for the children.
7. He gets into trouble.
8. Answers may vary – perhaps the children's mother says 'Bad' to Bones.
9. Answers may vary – he is probably trustworthy and friendly.
10. Answers may vary – he may have got his name because he likes bones.

Narrative

6 **The first chick**

Question types: 2 literal, 2 deductive, 2 inferential, 2 evaluative
1. Otto was bouncing on Claudius's feet and waving his flippers.
2. Otto wanted to fly.
3. Penguins use their flippers to swim.
4. The skua was looking for food.
5. Answers may vary – Antarctica.
6. Otto was puzzled that both Claudius and the skua liked chicks, but the skua was 'nasty'.
7and 8. Own answers.

7 **The Owl Who Was Afraid of the Dark**

Question types: 2 literal, 2 inferential, 2 evaluative, 2 deductive
1. Plop was a Barn Owl.
2. Plop didn't like the dark.
3. Owls are called night birds because they are most active at night.
4. Mrs Barn Owl will need patience to get Plop used to the dark.
5. Plop wants to be a day bird because he doesn't like the dark.
6. Own answer.
7. Plop is only a baby and hasn't been out of the nest yet.
8. Own answer.

8 **Ursula Bear**

Question types: 2 literal, 2 inferential, 2 evaluative, 2 deductive
1. Ursula was very fond of bears.
2. Ursula had been to a dancing lesson.
3. Own answer.
4. The poster could be advertising a circus.
5. Own answer.
6. She got flour on her nose when she was making gingerbread.
7. Being a bear had got her into trouble.
8. It was easy to turn into a bear.

9 **The Twits**

Question types: 2 literal, 2 inferential, 2 evaluative, 2 deductive
1. The Twits had Bird Pie for supper on Wednesdays.
2. Mr Twit climbed into The Big Dead Tree.
3. Mr Twit put glue on the branches on Tuesday, the day before Bird Pie day.
4. The birds wanted to rest for the night.
5. Own answer.
6. He saw the birds roosting on the branches and thought glue would be a good way to catch them.
7. Mrs Twit would have to pluck the feathers off.
8. Own answer.

10 **A Birthday for Frances**

Question types: 2 literal, 2 inferential, 2 evaluative, 2 deductive
1. Mother and Gloria were sitting at the table.
2. Frances was in the broom cupboard.
3. Frances is older than Gloria.
4. Alice is not a real person.
5. No one can see Alice because she is not real.
6. Frances uses the letters to spell cake and candy because she cannot spell yet.
7. Answers may vary – 'candy' and 'closet' suggest that it is American.
8. Own answer.

11 **No Roses for Harry**

Question types: 2 literal, 3 inferential, 3 evaluative, 2 deductive
1. Harry was a white dog with black spots.
2. Grandma gave Harry the sweater.
3. Own answer
4. It was nice and warm.
5. People kept finding the sweater and giving it back to Harry.
6. They didn't want Harry to lose the sweater.
7. Answers may vary – perhaps Harry didn't feel like playing with his friends because he was wearing the sweater that he didn't like, and he must have been feeling tired after trying so hard to lose it on the shopping trip.
8. Own answer.
9. No, Harry didn't mean the bird to take the wool.
10. Own answer.

12 **Charlie and the Chocolate Factory**

Question types: 2 literal, 3 inferential, 2 evaluative, 3 deductive
1. The room was like a gigantic witch's kitchen.
2. He was excited because it was his favourite room.
3. The delicious rich smells were being made by the mixtures cooking.
4. He couldn't decide which to look at first.
5. She thought an Everlasting Gobstopper was like chewing gum because it lasted a long time.
6. The Everlasting Gobstoppers lasted for ever so they wouldn't need to buy another.
7 and 8. Own answers.
9. Yes, he stared around it.
10. It was a hard, round, green ball, the same size and shape as a marble.

Drama

13 Treasure trove

Question types: 2 literal, 2 inferential, 2 evaluative, 2 deductive
1. The boys were playing football.
2. Will had kicked the ball over the hedge.
3. The dagger punctured the ball.
4. They took their find to the police station because it was probably valuable.
5. If it had been put there on purpose and if it were solid silver, it would be a treasure trove.
6 and 7. Own answers.
8. 'Solid silver' means that the things were made of pure silver.

Recount

14 My new school

Question types: 2 literal, 2 inferential, 2 deductive, 2 evaluative
1. The writer's dad is a policeman.
2. His new job is in Dorset.
3. The writer is a girl.
4. It means, 'Where do you live?'
5 and 6. Own answers.
7. If Selina comes round for tea it will show the writer wants to be friends.
8. The writer can join the recorder group and make more friends.

Instructions

15 Fruit and cheese kebabs

Question types: 2 literal, 2 inferential, 2 evaluative, 2 deductive
1. The shopping list would be: cheese of different types, green and black grapes, pineapple chunks, mandarin oranges and cocktail sticks or kebab skewers.
2. Own answer.
3. The cheese needs to be firm to thread it on to the skewer.
4. You must always wash your hands.
5. Own answer.
6. You could use apple, celery or cucumber.
7. The grapes may be dusty or dirty or may have been sprayed with pesticides.
8. If the grapes and fruit were wet they would spoil the cheese.

16 First aid for a grazed knee

Question types: 3 literal, 2 inferential, 1 evaluative, 2 deductive
1. You could fall and slide along the ground.
2. The graze would be sore.
3. You need warm water, cotton wool balls, sterile gauze and adhesive tape or dressings.
4. Own answer.
5. 'Germ free' means the same as sterile.
6. The graze could get infected.
7. Own answer.
8. You should dial 999 for an ambulance.

Report

17 Dunston Primary School PTA

Question types: 2 literal, 2 inferential, 3 evaluative, 2 deductive
1. PTA stands for Parent-Teacher Association.
2. The PTA organised six events.
3. Own answer.
4. The barn dance made £646 altogether.
5. The barn dance made the most money.
6. A lifeguard is needed for safety.
7. A parent who is interested in the school would belong to the PTA.
8 and 9. Own answers.

18 The playground

Question types: 2 literal, 2 inferential, 2 evaluative, 2 deductive
1. A reporter for a local paper writes about things that have happened in the area.
2. A new slide and playhouse are next to the sandpit.
3. Children over 14 years could break the equipment.
4. The rubber tiles are to stop children hurting themselves.
5 and 6. Own answers.
7. Dunston County Council looks after the playground.
8. The money came from the National Lottery.

Explanation

19 Toothpaste

Question types: 2 literal, 2 inferential, 2 evaluative, 2 deductive
1. Toothpaste was made of ground-up burnt eggshells, cuttlefish bone or coral.
2. Bacteria in plaque can decay teeth.
3. The grit scrapes away the layer on our teeth left by food and drink.
4. Answers may vary – probably no, because fluoride in toothpaste helps to prevent our teeth decaying.
5. Foam gets in between the teeth.
6. Own answer.
7. Sticky sweets will leave a sticky layer on our teeth.
8. The outside layer of a tooth is made of enamel.

20 Water

Question types: 2 literal, 2 inferential, 2 evaluative, 4 deductive
1. We use water for washing machines, dishwashers, showers, baths and lavatories.
2. The water comes from the rain.
3. We use water to drink, cook, clean our teeth and water indoor plants.
4. There would be no water.
5. There might be fish, chemicals and rubbish in the river.
6. We might get ill.
7. Own answer.
8. We would need to take out the salt.
9. Own answer.
10. A reservoir is used to store water.

21 ### The library

Question types: 2 literal, 2 inferential, 2 evaluative, 2 deductive
1. Local people in the area would use the public library.
2. A collection of books is called a library.
3. Melvil Dewey put non-fiction books into subject groups.
4. A book about computers is non-fiction.
5. A Dewey number tells you what subject group the book is in.
6. Non-fiction books have been grouped by subject for 126 years. (Note: answer will alter depending on the present year.)
7 and 8. Own answers.

Argument

22 ### Early to bed

Question types: 2 literal, 2 inferential, 2 evaluative, 2 deductive
1. They make a fuss when they are told to go to bed.
2. Young children need twelve hours sleep per night.
3. Answers may vary – children may want to keep on playing or watching TV.
4. The brain gets tired from working all day.
5. Answers may vary – people who are tired could drop things and make mistakes.
6. No, an adult's skeleton is hard.
7 and 8. Own answer.

23 ### Dental hygiene

Question types: 2 literal, 2 inferential, 3 evaluative, 3 deductive
1. A baby's first teeth are called milk teeth.
2. The teeth will decay.
3. Our teeth grind up our food to make it easier to swallow and digest.
4. Rinsing your teeth will wash out the food and drink left in your mouth.
5 and 6. Own answers.
7. If a tooth decayed it would hurt and you would have to have a filling or even have the tooth taken out.
8. Own answer.
9. They are called milk teeth because they come when babies are still fed on milk.
10. If the teeth are brushed from side to side the bristles of the toothbrush cannot clean between the teeth.

24 ### Saving wild flowers

Question types: 2 literal, 3 inferential, 1 evaluative, 2 deductive
1. Dandelions, daisies, sowthistles and buttercups are unlikely to become extinct.
2. The farmers think of the wild flowers as weeds.
3. Own answer.
4. They can have part of their garden as a wild garden.
5. The rarer flowers do not like all soils.
6. A gardener might find the rarer wild flowers will not grow.
7. People who pick the wild flowers could cause them to disappear.
8. You could look around the area to see which wild flowers are already growing well, and where.